Narcolepsy Falls Asleep

by
Richard E Friesen

In which Narcolepsy learns the value of
narcolepsy

1
Coitus Interruptus

Donelle Mars walked through a strange landscape, a gravel yard between a ranch-style house, a red barn, and a metal building. A few trees grew behind the house, and metal fencing ran between the barn and the steel building. The dim light reminded her of a long summer twilight, but they'd had a wet spring snow the day before. Manure and diesel smoke stank up the air, with aromas of soup and peanut butter overpowering it all. On the porch, a boy sat in a glider chair, eating spoonfuls of peanut butter from a jar.

Blinking, Donelle looked up at the cotton-candy-clouds—pink, with stringy stuff winding around white cones. Now they just needed tangerine trees and marmalade skies. Oh, lord, she was dreaming someone else's dream. She'd never even visited a farm. How could she know what one looked like?

She'd had such a delightful day too. Samuel had taken her to brunch. They'd walked in the park, wonderful even with the chill and damp. Back in his apartment, they'd kissed on the couch before moving to the bed. Donelle had ribbed him about his one-room place, but stopped, kneeling on the bed with her blouse half-unbuttoned. "Are you sure you want to do this?"

Laying down, he put hands behind his head. "I hoped, that as a wicked divorced woman, you would ravish me, overcoming the shame and guilt visited upon me by my parents in my childhood."

"Hey, only I can call myself that. Besides, you're hopeless." Donelle dismissed him with a wave and turned to go.

Sam leaped up, grabbed her around the waist, and pulled her down backward on atop him. "Not so fast! You have to experience the guilt and shame first. It's like a disease. It rubs off."

Donelle had laid her head back beside Sam's as he kissed her neck and caressed her. He proved an earnest lover, taking his time on the foreplay. When they got down to it, Sam had closed his eyes and…

Before she could draw a conclusion, an old pickup with a border collie riding in back rattled up the gravel drive and came to a stop beside the barn. The dog barked at Donelle once, jumped down, and bounded toward her. With each leap, it grew. When it reached her, its doggy-breath washed over her, and it licked her face without jumping. Its slobber coated her nose and cheek. Laughing and sputtering, Donelle tried to push the beast away. Instead, she ended up on her back, dog beside her licking her all over. It tickled, making Donelle howl and squirm. Wrestling with the dog, it's fur warm against her skin, left her breathless and excited.

Before she could get free, a shrill voice with no source echoed across the landscape. "Samuel Elijah Neufeld! What do you think you're doing?

The dog yelped, it's tail drooped, and it lay down, furry side against her skin.

Wait. Where had her clothes gone?

Donelle woke with a start, laying on Samuel, right where she'd moved when they finished the foreplay. Sure enough, his eyes fluttered too, waking. Lifting herself on one hand, she smacked his chest. "You fell asleep while making love to me! Do I mean that little to you?" Slapping his chest again, Donelle rolled off him and leaped from the bed.

"Donelle, wait! I'm sorry! I didn't mean…"

Not bothering with underwear, Donelle pulled on her shirt and pants, stuffed panties in her purse and stormed out, slamming the little apartment's door behind her. As soon as she could no longer hear Sam's voice, she regretted her anger. After all, she'd fallen asleep too. How bizarre. The dream resonated with a video she'd seen about Metallo and Scream, two superheroes in New York—perhaps the weirdness. Who had that voice been? It sounded like a mother.

~~~~

Samuel Neufeld pounded the sheets in frustration. "Damn, damn, damn," Why did he always fall asleep? After laying on his back staring at the textured, white ceiling until his breathing calmed, Sam rolled off the bed. Not bothering with clothes, he padded over to the tiny kitchen and poured some trail mix into his hand.

As he munched, he wondered if Donelle would ever speak to him again. His heart clogged up his throat, and he had to swallow hard to get the raisins, chocolate, and almonds down. Why had his eyes closed? Why had his half-conscious mind conjured his uncle's old farm? Why their first time? He hadn't even had a chance to speak to Donelle before she shrank as he bounded over to her. The wrestling and licking had been strange and fun. Compared to his other experience, the entire day had been marvelous. What would have happened next, if his mom hadn't shown up?

Frustrated with himself and worried Donelle wouldn't be back, Sam picked up some gym shorts from the floor and pulled them on before skirting the couch and turning on his TV. Sam found his training videos for Krav Maga, a mixed martial art created by the Israeli army. He never expected to use it, but it kept him in shape, and it had a cool name.

Hoping the physicality would clear his mind, he followed the instructor through the simple, practical forms. On a move where he had to hold the position for a few seconds, Sam's eyes drooped and the room became a highway at night, white stripes flashing by. A big purple ball bounced in front of him, dropping money on the ground as it went.

Sam shook himself awake. Angry, he jabbed the buttons on the remote to stop the video. He'd asked the damned doctor, gotten medicine, and nothing helped. To think it had all started by falling asleep in his college classes.

Needing to work off his frustration, Sam donned a T-shirt, hoodie, and running shoes. He couldn't fall asleep while running. As he headed out, he grabbed his keys and said, "Alexa, lock the door behind me."

"Yes, Sam."

Rather than wait for the elevator, he jogged down the stairs. When he burst into the dark, chilly evening, he took a big breath of the Rocky Mountain air, mixed with a little car exhaust. The wind bit at his exposed legs, but they would get hot soon enough. He used the block and half north to Sloan Lake to warm up. When he crossed 17th into the park, he stopped to stretch calves and hamstrings, thinking about Donelle's smile and her sardonic wit. Few could match her intelligence, and he'd screwed it up.

He took off, an initial sprint to burn off the anger. Not that his sprints had much speed. He'd never been a sprinter. On his high school track team, he could run a long way without slowing much, but when they'd asked to run the 400 in medley relay, he'd taken the baton in first place and given it to the anchor leg runner in last. The two and half miles around Sloan Lake would just get him warmed up.

When he reached the tennis courts, a woman with an athletic stroller jogged toward him. A man dashed out from the courts and grabbed her large purse, knocking her down in the process. The woman cried out as she fell, but the thief ran straight toward Sam.

Sam got up on his toes, and stepped into the thief's path before his pacifist upbringing reared its head. He decided to try reason first. "Give the lady back her purse."

"Fuck off!" The teenage thief veered into the grass to go around Sam.

So much for the nice approach. Time to find if his Krav Maga martial arts worked worth shit. How did grappling fit with being a pacifist? Stepping in front of the thief, he tried for a throw. The kid ran right past him. Sam grabbed him and held on. The kid dragged him down the path.

Stumbling and staggering to keep up, Sam's eyes drooped. He tried to blink, to stay awake. He couldn't fall asleep now! His eyes closed again, and his brain fired random thoughts about work. The park trees turned into the haunted woods from the Wizard of Oz—gnarled boles, howling wind, and flying monkeys.

The thief fell to the ground then looked around, dumbfounded.

Sam let go and sat up. "Hey, monkeys! The witch wants this guy!"

The thief looked up, eyes wide, as five flying monkeys swooped down to carry him away. They lifted him off the ground and flapped up through the leafless branches. The thief struggled and tore at their claws until they dropped him—from thirty feet.

He landed on a perfect pillow pile, bounced and groaned. Sam sat down next to the kid to cover the childhood heebie-jeebies shaking in his chest. "Interesting choice. I would have given the purse back, myself."

Overhead, monkeys circled, screaming. The light grew dimmer, as if smoke blew across the sun. The kid just stared.

"Ah, well. I suppose I should let them have you." Sam rolled to his feet and stepped away.

The monkeys dropped from the sky and latched onto the would-be thief. He screamed as they lifted him again. "Help me!"

Sam cocked his head. "Are you going to give the purse back and apologize?"

A voice came from nowhere. "I called the…" The woman who belonged to the purse appeared. "…cops." She looked around at the haunted forest. "What the hell?"

"It's the haunted forest. Dorothy and the Tinman ought to be along soon." The yellow brick road appeared beneath their feet. "Then we can all go off to see the wizard."

Both the woman and the thief stared at him like a crazy man. Maybe he was. How did they get in his dream? Sam decided to go with it. What could be more insane than a dream? "It's the dragon you have to watch out for." He pointed at the sky as a shadow flew over them.

"There's no dragon in Wizard of Oz," the thief cried.

The woman cowered under a tree. Sam walked over to her. "Don't worry. He's not coming for you."

Far away voices sang, "We're off to see the wizard, the wonderful Wizard of Dreams." The haunted forest faded away to reveal cornfields. A rather non-descript Dorothy appeared on the road with the Tinman. This Tinman wore a police hat and confusion on his face. "What the hell?"

"Welcome to the game!" Sam shouted as munchkins in football pads bumped and bounced out onto the field. "Everyone, huddle up."

The confused thief, the woman, the tinman-cop, and indistinct Dorothy gathered close. Sam knelt and gave them the play, pointing at the woman first. "You go long. Dorothy, cut across to take the defenders with you. You two guys block the munchkins. On three." Since he'd touched them all to get them here, touching to get back made sense. He held his hand out for them to grab. When they did, he said, "Ready, wake!"

Sam blinked and found himself back in Sloan Lake park, with the thief, the victim, and a police officer lying on him. "Ugh. I had the strangest dream, Aunty Em. You were in it, and you were in it, even you."

All three glared, puzzled and angry, the officer finished handcuffing the thief and hauled him to his feet. His name tag read "Willis." Looking between the woman, Sam, and the thief, he tried to recover his severe, in-control attitude. "What's happening here?"

Sam pointed at the thief. "He stole this woman's—"

"Diaper bag," she interrupted. "He stole my diaper bag."

Everyone looked over at the stolen bag, which had spilled its contents—diapers, wipes, a Ziploc with Cheerios, and lotion.

Three hours later, Sam staggered into his apartment. The police had grilled him, even as they praised him for helping. The perpetrator's story confused them, what with flying monkeys, haunted forests, and munchkin football. Sergeant Willis stayed mum, so they gave the thief a psych eval. Sam stuck with his judo hold story and landing on the guy by accident.

Exhausted, Sam went through his bedtime rituals—brushing teeth, washing his face, and putting on pajamas. When he laid down and pulled the sheet across his skin, Sam stared up at the ceiling, wide awake. He tried to calm his breathing. He rolled to his side and closed his eyes. A song from the police station radio played in his head. He squirmed until his eyes popped open again. During the day, at work, making love, he fell asleep. Lying in bed, his mind raced. Groaning in disgust, he threw the sheet off and got up. Maybe working out again would help. What had he just done with those people in the dream? What did it mean?

2
Dream Power

The next day, in the IT Infrastructure staff meeting at the hospital, Sam worried about his job. He'd left a Fortune 500 company after two years to take a job here in the hospital. He wanted to help people rather than make some rich guy richer. He'd still fallen asleep in the meeting. This time his boss hadn't said a word. He'd just given Sam a disappointed head shake.

Later, Sam trudged into the little break room—one round table, coffee machine, fridge, and microwave—to eat his lunch. The leftover pork chops and grilled vegetables reminded him Donelle had stormed out.

After foiling a robbery yesterday, today should have been a good day. But even when he tried to help, it didn't work out.

Sara, the network engineer, walked in and warmed up her lunch. "Hi, Sam. Did you see what happened in New York this morning?"

"No."

Unconcerned if Sam wanted to see, she got out her phone and brought up a shaky video. It looked like a bank lobby. A large, purple guy, the color of a child holding his breath too long, tucked into a ball and crashed in through the revolving door, leaving a metal pretzel and shattered glass on the floor. He bounced once and somersaulted through the plexiglass that shielded the tellers, taking the entire bullet-proof sheet with him. One more bounce and he crashed into the vault door, which crumpled like so much tinfoil. He stood up, walked into the vault, and came back out with armfuls of money bags. Two bank guards ordered the purple thief to stop. When he didn't, they shot him—four times each. The Purple Bouncer didn't notice. The bullets bounced as if hitting a rubber ball, and he kept bouncing.

"Can you believe that? He just demolished the vault!" Sara said.

The person with the phone dashed to the bank windows, making a nauseating ride.

"Watch this, watch this!" Sara said, bouncing in her seat.

Sam leaned forward, tense. A SWAT unit had arrived outside, but their bullets didn't work any better than the guards' had.

A man and a woman came down from the sky. It looked like the woman held the man in the air. She landed on a fire hydrant, dropping the man to the sidewalk. They both wore silly spandex suits. The masks didn't help. The woman yelled at the Purple Bouncer to stop, but he ignored her. Instead, the Purple Bouncer bounced over a police cruiser, but the woman lifted the car from ten yards away and slammed it into Purple. He bounced higher.

The spandex man opened his mouth and screamed. Car windows exploded. Police officers fell to the ground, holding their heads. The Purple Bouncer threw the money and put his hands over his ears. He hopped toward the spandex pair, bouncing up into a graceful arc aimed right at them.

Spandex-man screamed again, and the woman threw another car. Neither stopped Purple. Spandex-man grabbed the woman, and she lifted them down the street, arcing back out of view from the window, but Purple bounced after them, like a big rubber ball.

Sam leaned closer. He'd left the money behind. A bag must have broken, because the wind following the bouncer carried flying bills. The watching crowd grabbed for the twenties as they went by.

"Who are the spandex twins?" Sam asked.

"What? Oh, uh, Metallo and Scream," Sara said. "The purple guy is the interesting one."

Sara knew their names. They'd been in the news before, and Donelle had mentioned them too. How had he missed all this?

After lunch, Sam kept drifting off at his desk, so he worked late to make sure he got the new servers built. He didn't leave until everyone else in the IT area had gone.

When Sam got off the elevator in his apartment building, Donelle stood in the hall with a Sidewok Café bag. His gut unclenched, his breathing eased, his heart stopped thumping, and some hairs laid back down. He hadn't even recognized the stress. He'd texted her three times and gotten no answer. Donelle had been waiting a while, but she'd stayed. Sam stopped five feet away. "Are you angry?"

She smirked. "At you being late? No. At you falling asleep? A little." She held up the bag. "I have...um...cold Chinese."

Sam closed the distance between them and kissed her cheek. "That's thoughtful, thanks." The door unlocked for him, his security system recognizing his face. Sam took the food from her, opened the apartment and walked in.

Donelle looked up at the tiny camera above the door. "That's...disturbing."

Turning, Sam followed her gaze and chuckled. She'd never seen his security system before. He'd always been inside to open the door. "It's a toy, mostly. I'm a computer guy, so I buy cool stuff and see what it can do." He set the bag on the counter, then leaned back to see Donelle around the corner. "Would you like me to add you, so you don't have to wait outside next time?"

She stared, mouth open, which told Sam how much he'd dared. A shiver ran down his spine.

Recovering, Donelle came over, kissed his cheek and wrapped her arms around his waist from behind. "You are so sweet. Let's see how the night unfolds."

Her body felt warm and delicious against his. Placing his hands over her arms, Sam laid his head back against hers. "The food's already cold. Want to eat later?"

"I should have brought pizza." Breaking away, Donelle went to sit on the bed. "I am mad at you for falling asleep our first time, but I fell asleep too."

Changing his mind, Sam plated the food and tossed it in the microwave. "As bad as I am at falling asleep, it was bound to happen. I wish it hadn't been the first time."

Laughing, Donelle patted the bed beside her. "I learned one thing in my short marriage. Sex is rarely what we expect. You have to go with the flow."

Sam went to join her on the bed and they watched the microwave count down. Sam sighed in contentment and frustration both and leaned against Donelle. "Not sure improvising is my forte."

She laughed even harder. "I would be happy to teach you."

They sat on the couch to eat. A little later, they turned off the TV and made out for a while. With Sam's hand under Donelle's shirt, she moaned into his mouth. The shame pounded into him as a child—sex is evil—rose its ugly head and warred with his lizard brain that wanted to jump her right then. For him, everything had changed when he had sex with his high school girlfriend and accidentally got her pregnant. They hadn't really known what sex was, though that didn't stop them feeling guilty for reaching under clothes. Her hypocrite, pro-life parents had sent her away to get an abortion. If, rather than portraying sex as evil, someone had explained what to do with a condom, they might have avoided all that pain. The whole incident had put Sam on a journey to a revised, kinder faith.

Donelle pulled back and gave him half a smile. "Should we feel guilty?"

She could also read his mind. They had met at church, but with neither of them virgins it hadn't taken long to get here. Sam bent down and kissed her soft, delicious lips and spoke into her mouth. "Should? No. Do? A little." She laid back on the couch, inviting him with her smile.

He slid over her, but as he nibbled her neck, his eyes drooped. No, not again. He fought to stay awake.

Donelle stroked his hair. "Ssh. It's okay. Go with it."

Her quiet words made him relax, but did she mean him to…

Sam stood on a muddy riverbank, his bare toes partway in the purple water. Large birds circled overhead in the kaleidoscope sky.

"Hey, Stranger. Come here often?" Donelle said.

"Well, not exactly here."

With a smile, she pressed her body into his and kissed him. When she pulled back, she cocked her head. "You saw me with the dog, didn't you?"

Sam's face grew hot. "I, um, yes. You mean, you...?"

With her arms around his neck, Donelle chuckled. "I haven't been tickled like that in ages." She stepped back and looked him over. "Why are we standing in mud? Doesn't mud wrestling involve two women?"

Tempted to create another woman, Sam instead took her hand. "Let's walk." Did he control his dreams? If so, what would Donelle like? Maybe an ocean would be nice.

They went squishing through the riverbank until it turned into a bank lobby, from which a yellow, or maybe gold, brick road led them to a sandy beach with waves crashing onto the violet land. The breakers made no sound, and the surf had no smell, but the sparkling water stretched into the distance where sea and sky blurred together.

After looking around, Donelle turned to hold both his hands. "You've never been to the ocean, have you?" Without waiting for an answer, she kissed him.

Mom's voice echoed over the beach. "Samuel Elijah Neufeld! Take your hands off that woman!"

Donelle pulled back and raised an eyebrow.

Would she leave him again? "I told you the shame is rather never ending, because sex is evil, of course. That's my mom. I wouldn't be surprised if my dad's voice comes in here too."

A mischievous smile blooming on her face, Donelle stepped back. It took her maybe a second and a half to lose her bikini. Where had the bikini even come from? With the smile daring the voices to object, she wiggled her hips, stuck out her chest and tongue while turning a circle, relishing her own body.

As Sam stepped up to her, wrapping her in his arms from behind, his father's voice broke the beach's silence. "Any woman who tempts my son is evil." When Sam didn't stop his caresses, his father added. "I'm ashamed to call you my son."

Donelle put her arms around his neck. "We should make our own noise."

~~~~

Later, when they woke up, Donelle stroked his hair and wrapped him in her legs. "A much better dream than last time."

Puzzled, Sam frowned. "You aren't mad?"

Sitting Sam up, Donelle sat up and a wry smile grew on her face. "Today, my firm got a new client—a would-be purse snatcher thwarted by a passerby. He had the strangest story about a man attacking him, then flying monkeys and munchkin football. I saw your name on the police report. Nice job, but you fell asleep, didn't you?"

Sam laid his forehead against hers. "Yes."

She put fingers under his chin and pulled his face up to look in his eyes. "You dope, that's your superpower."

"My what?"

She smacked his forehead with her palm. "Pay attention. Do you think just anyone can be grappling with a thief and fall asleep? That doesn't even count the silent beach and flying monkeys."

Sam blinked, trying to digest the idea. "I…you mean I have a real superpower, like the Purple Bouncer?"

Donelle gave him a peck on the lips. "Yes. If you can hang on to him, you can beat him."

"Yeah, if he doesn't squash me." Sam reached out to caress her. "How do you even become a superhero? I mean, I'd have to know when a crime happens and go find it. If I drive, it could take half an hour or more to get there. Do I have to wear spandex?"

What did it mean to be a hero? He didn't want to hurt anyone, not even to fight if he could avoid it. He would make a strange hero.

Pushing him over, she tried to lay on him. Instead, she teetered and pulled him onto the floor. Somehow, she landed on top. "Oof," Sam said. His elbow hit a box of take-out Chinese, scattering rice over them and the couch.

"That's supposed to wait for a wedding." Donelle picked rice out of her hair, then got back to the subject at hand. "Of course you need a costume. It tells the police what to expect. It's like if you ride a road bike, you have to have a bike suit with ads on it, like you're in the Tour de France. Besides, I want to see your cute ass in spandex."

With one hand, Sam pulled her down toward him. He kissed her throat. "Maybe this time I can stay awake."

Ten minutes later, Sam stood on a high ledge with a temple door leading into the cliff behind him. Donelle, naked and sexy, stood hands on hips, torn between glaring and grinning.

Sam tried the door—locked, of course. Looking at his arms, he wondered if he could add muscles. Even as his arms ballooned to ridiculous portions, he turned to the door and shrugged. "Sam smash!"

"Wrong guy," Donelle said, laughing.

3
The Other Guys

Jenna smiled when Noah walked into the Holiday Inn near Midway airport in Chicago. She'd waited for him in the lobby, drinking coffee and surfing the net. The place had that sterile-comfy look favored by all mid-priced hotels. No one there had given Jenna a second look. Even Noah hadn't noticed.

Jenna rose and dropped her "don't notice me" Zen as Noah walked by. "Boo!"

Noah jumped and breathed in, skin tinging purple before he stopped himself. Then his face lit, and he reached out. She led him to the elevator without touching him, wondering if he might treat her the way a brother should.

He didn't talk until the elevator doors closed. "I thought the grunting and smashing went well, until bitch and bastard showed up. At least they couldn't hurt me."

"Don't sell yourself short. Chasing them and taking all the attention with you was brilliant." It had even let her scatter the contents of one bag so all the ordinary people could benefit, not as much as her and Noah, but benefit still. They got off on the fourth floor and she led him to 423. She even handed him a key card.

When they walked in, each double bed had a full bank bag from New York laying on it. Noah laughed and hefted one. "You picked these up and walked away?" He stepped over and tried to kiss her.

Jenna pushed him away. "I told you, I'm not interested. Stop trying." A real brother wouldn't do that, though hers had.

Taking a step back, Noah turned purple and bounced between floor and ceiling, cracking the plaster. He stopped, shook himself, and exhaled. A stench rolled through the room.

Jenna waved her hand. "Oh, God. Don't do that!"

Noah ignored her, opened the bag, and pulled out tens and twenties in packets. "We would have had four times this much if those two hadn't shown up. What's next?"

Sitting in the desk chair, Jenna spun it around. "How about we put it all in a Panamanian bank?"

Noah laughed. "So someone can steal it? That doesn't sound good."

With a smile, Jenna shook her head. "Only if they're hackers." Jenna blinked. "Let's hit some small-town places going south. At each one we first deposit money, then transfer it to Panama. The next day we steal the cash back. After a bit, we stop doing any jobs and turn west, to throw off the feds. Colorado, I think."

Noah sat on the bed. "Sure. Let's stop by my parent's place in Kansas for a bit. We should smash up some mansions too. You need some jewelry if you're going to be an island queen. But let's start with an armored car. There are a few costumed clowns around here too, so we make it fast. We need to find a way for Big, Bouncy, and Distracting to let you get a bigger haul. Maybe you need a truck to carry the loot."

"You want me to drive a semi?" Jenna got out her laptop and researched which banks had foreclosed on the most homes. One would surely have an armored car service.

The next day, in late afternoon, an armored car drove down Kirk Road toward Butterfield, where some construction had blocked off a lane with concrete barriers. In a Starbucks parking lot, Jenna sat in a stolen Jeep with a lifted suspension, engine running, savoring a strawberry Frappuccino. A thrill shot through Jenna as a purple blur came from the roof and landed in front of the armored car. The road split with a crack as he bounced right into the trucks armored grill. It rang like a bell.

The ironclad vehicle crumpled. Steam hissed from the radiator. Jenna wished she could destroy things like Noah. The man had to be as dense as plutonium. The freaked-out drivers shot at him, to little effect. Noah bounced off a concrete barrier in front to send him over the truck. There he used the curb and his legs to reverse direction and smash the back door of the armored car. The guard in back shot him too, but then jumped out and ran away.

Rather than going in, Noah bounced from barrier to armored truck again. He bashed in the driver's door, grabbed the guard and tossed him into the street. Cars screeched to a halt, adding burnt rubber to the street smells. People pulled out their phones to record Noah. He bounced into a nearby car, shoving it aside as if clearing a space. Its airbags deployed with a loud pop.

Jenna loved watching Noah destroy things, but she still calmed her breathing and cleared her mind, letting all the day's trouble flow through her, along with everyone's attention. Cameras might find her later, but with Noah attracting all the attention, it didn't matter much. She'd never tried to hide a car before, but this time, she believed she had. The sensation of other eyes on her faded, even the sound of her own breathing muted, so she drove the lifted Jeep forward, bumping over a curb, through two bushes and one small tree, jostling her back and forth. When she bounced down onto the street, she pulled right up to the armored car's rear door. It took no effort at all to crawl out the passenger door, into the truck, and grab all the money bags. One she cut open with a knife and tossed out toward Starbucks. The people needed the money more than the banks. Bills scattered on the wind.

Maintaining her calm Zen state, Jenna got in the Jeep and drove away, weaving through the traffic jam, over the median and into the now-empty northbound lanes. She wanted to stay and watch Noah bounce, but she kept to the plan and turned into the Walmart parking lot to wait.

The trickiest part always came with Noah making his escape. If he waited too long, police helicopters and news choppers would show up, making the whole thing near impossible. Purple did not escape notice. Noah took a big leap, bounced on a car and over the Starbucks. The next bouncing leap took him up and over the Walmart. He didn't come back up again.

Anyone on the big store's far side might have noticed him come down in an alcove by the trash bins. Noah planned to deflate and walk around the building to the parking lot. As long as no one saw where he'd come from, he'd stroll out to the Jeep like any other customer.

When Noah opened the passenger door, Jenna jumped. He grinned as she cranked the engine and drove away like a little old granny.

Noah asked, "How many bags did you get?"

"Nine. Is that better?"

"Much better. Now we just have to launder the cash through a bank or two. It's like recycling, and we have to do our part to save the planet."

Depositing money, transferring it, and stealing back the cash, couldn't really be called laundering, but it made the discussion shorter. She would get enough money that no one would be able to hurt her ever again. Ever.

4
Training Day

Sam, wearing his new gi, bowed to his new Krav Maga martial arts instructor. Did everything have a uniform? Donelle said you couldn't ride a bicycle without the outfit. Sam had paid for real training after the near fiasco with the would-be purse-snatcher, real private training. When he walked out onto the mat, the teacher, Ray Elegion, folded his arms. "You fell asleep over there." The man had lean muscles and a shaved head to go with his mustache and bulbous nose.

Glancing back at the bench where he'd waited for the day's last regular class to end, Sam shrugged. "Yes. I have narcolepsy. No disrespect intended." Sam considered. "I would like to pay for discretion too."

Ray blinked. "No charge, if that's what you need, I'll keep quiet." He gestured Sam closer. "Show me what you know."

Stepping closer, Sam judged what to do against an expert. "There is one more thing…well, you'll find out." He went for a leg sweep, anticipating the counter. When Ray jumped over and struck back, Sam grabbed his arm and went for a hold. Ray reversed it and flipped Sam over his shoulder. On the way down, Sam's eyes drooped shut.

He hit the ground in a high school corridor, linoleum tiles, and walls lined with lockers, doors, and spirit posters. He'd just been tripped by some bully. Faceless students shuffled past his prone figure on their imaginary day.

Ray rushed by. "I'm late for class!" Five steps away he stopped. "What the fuck?" He turned back to Sam. "I've forgotten what class, even where it is. I just know there's a class I need to get to. That's not right."

"Welcome to my dream." He reached up and laid a hand on Ray's calf, magically closing the distance between them without moving. "How about we wake up?"

Sam opened his eyes with Ray lying across him, as if he'd collapsed doing a throw.

Ray groaned, scrambled to his feet, and backed away. "What the hell?"

Sitting up, Sam smiled. "I told you, I have narcolepsy, with a twist."

Staring, Ray didn't speak until his breathing calmed. He sank down to the mat, cross-legged. "You fell asleep while…" He gestured to one side. "And we went…shit."

Taking a long breath, Sam told Ray what he needed. "Someone suggested I could help with the rather odd criminals showing up these days."

"Oh, like Purple and Bouncy!"

Sam laughed. "He won the Internet that day, didn't he?"

"He did." Ray pursed his lips. "So, you need two things. First, not to get dead before you fall asleep, and second, to hold on so you can drag them into your dream when you do fall asleep." When Sam nodded, Ray shrugged and got to his feet. "We'd best get started. This should be interesting. The problem is, you can't learn it without actual holds and throws. The moves aren't enough."

"It shouldn't be a problem, as long as you don't mind a little dreaming."

~~~~

A few days later, Sam stood before a police sergeant, feeling like an idiot. He'd whined about the dark gray spandex suit Donelle made him wear. "Come on, Donelle. No one looks good in spandex. Just look at all the guys on bicycles! These sunglasses and scarf make me look like an old-west bandit. Do I have to go out in this?"

"Yes. Don't you ever read comics? Did you ever see a hero without a suit and catchy name? I'll get you a real mask later."

Sam had donned a jacket and sweat pants over the silly costume. Donelle had used her contacts to finagle him a police-ride-along.

At the station, the sergeant did not look impressed. Hands on hips, he paced, scowling. "I have no use for vigilantes in my city. *We* uphold the law. Idiots in masks and spandex break it. Our forefathers founded this country on the principles of law and order. No lone vigilante could live up to that. Never!" He put his finger in Sam's face. "Now get out there and fight crime."

Sam didn't know whether to laugh, give a history lesson, or try to explain himself. Did he even want to be a hero? He did want to help people, but would he have a chance at that? He opted for the minimum reply. "Yes, sir. I understand." He didn't want to hurt anyone, period, but saying so wouldn't help. How could he be a hero and not fight?

After more haranguing about law and order, the sergeant assigned him to Officer Stanislaw Johns for the ride-along. He had one last word for Sam as he sent them out. "Stay in the car."

How could he fight crime if he stayed in the car?

Before they'd reached the cruiser, Officer Johns had gone from a suppressed smile to outright laughing. Despite the name, Johns had an Asian look, with his jet hair pulled up into a man-bun. He even pulled it off.

He waved Sam over to ride shotgun. "Don't mind Sarge. He hates letting you come along, but those costumed clowns have him scared shitless. Getting one on our side will be good." Johns gave Sam a sidelong glance. "What is it you do, anyway?"

"Well, it's a little hard to explain." Sam didn't want to reveal his silly sleeping superpower and hear Johns laugh.

"One big question is, are you bulletproof? You can call me Officer Johns, or just Johns, by the way." He exited the garage and drove down the street. As they went, Johns watched left and right, looking for criminals.

"No, I'm not bulletproof. I'm taking mixed martial arts training. I don't know what will happen if I encounter a spandex criminal." Sam had no idea how this would go. The Purple

Bouncer scared him. "Are there any spandex criminals in Denver? I wouldn't mind trying this out."

"Rumors, but nothing concrete. What's the N for?"

Sam glanced at his chest. Donelle had put a stylized gray N on his suit. It shimmered in the dark squad car. Considering how the man might react, Sam shook his head. "I'll tell you later. What do we do now?"

"We could look for a white guy with his taillight out. That way we could shoot him and even up the odds a bit. I say 'I feared for my life,' and no one thinks twice."

Sam gaped until Officer Johns laughed and cuffed him. "Gotcha."

Forcing a laugh, Sam shook his head. Johns had a twisted, dark sense of humor. Sam tried his question again. "How does this work?"

Johns shrugged. "Like Sarge said, you stay in the car. We cruise around until we see someone breaking the law, or until dispatch sends us somewhere."

"So, it's boring."

"Truth? Those of us who want to protect people, like it boring."

Two hours later, they had issued a speeding ticket and caught a drunk driver. Near midnight, dispatch reported a loud party near the DU campus. "The rich boys again," Johns said with a head shake.

When they arrived at the house south of campus it looked like an ordinary college party—beer, loud music, shouting, and trash on the lawn. Another cruiser showed up at the same time, and the two officers got out with nightsticks ready. "All right, boys, party's over."

On a patio to one side, a girl shrieked and laughed. Three girls and two boys gathered around a little fire in a brazier. One boy, dressed in artfully casual clothes only the wealthy could afford, reached out to touch a girl's arm with two fingers. His hand blurred, and the girl pulled away, laughing and annoyed at the same time.

"Uh, oh." Sam leapt from the car. The kid's power looked harmless but might not be. The music quieted down so Sam could hear the next girl say, "I'm not ticklish."

The Tickler gave a predatory laugh and touched her cheek. "Of course you are."

The girl shied away, laughing in spite of herself. Tickler gave chase. He tickled her twice more until he ran into Officer Johns.

Johns grabbed the Tickler's shoulder. "Time to call it a night, young man."

The boy spun and reached out. Johns blocked with his nightstick. Tickler grabbed the baton and his hand shook. The plastic shaft vibrated, almost ripping itself from Officer Johns' hand. With a loud crack, it shattered and disintegrated to dust and splinters, raining to the ground.

Both stared at the shredded plastic. Sam ran toward them. How did he block a tickling hand? Treat it like a knife, maybe?

Anger darkened Officer Johns' face, and he reached for the boy. The Tickler laid a hand on Johns' shoulder. Sam grabbed the offending wrist and twisted. When the kid tried to touch him, Sam shifted his weight and threw the boy over his hip. Following him down, Sam held the vibrating hand at bay and took a deep breath.

He tried, but his eyes didn't droop.

The kid said, "Hey, get off me! What are you doing?"

This kid needed a lesson in more than just brains. "You need a lesson in manners. Now my mother taught me…" Sam's eyes fluttered shut.

Sam stood beside a bed, to which Tickler had been tied. The ropes wrapped around solid gold posts. "Well, isn't this kinky?" Moving closer, Sam's legs stirred up feathers—white ones, brown, blue, and red ones, Ostrich and sparrow sized ones. He picked up a striped hawk feather. "There's a saying, 'Do unto others what you would have them do unto you.' I assume, then, that you like to be tickled."

Before Sam could make a move, a bird squawked behind him. A chicken strutted atop the piled feathers. This one had extra plumage spiking out where its beak and feet should have been.

Shrugging, Sam picked the bird up and set it on Tickler's bare chest. The chicken strutted its way across the Tickler on its weird feathery feet.

The Tickler shrieked and laughed and squirmed, but he did not look happy, making Sam uncomfortable. Was this how a hero acted?

The chicken squawked again and grew larger. As it did, a human head peered out from the feathered face. Sergeant Willis, sitting on the Tickler and wearing a police hat, shook his head. "What the…I didn't touch you! Where are we?"

Sam looked around at the clouds where the room had been, wispy tendrils curling around their legs. Blue sky bloomed overhead.

Sergeant Willis's feathers drew back to form large, white wings. His white-feather robes flowed around him. The blue hat with gold braid didn't match. "Hey, I'm no angel!"

"Oh, right."

Willis's wings widened, and his body shortened as he became an eagle, still with his own head and a police hat. He looked at his new body and nodded. "Better."

The piled feathers vanished with the bed. A giant purple ball smashed into the gold bedposts, which shattered into coins. The Tickler floated on air, looking more terrified than when strapped and tickled. "Am I dead?"

Laughing, Sam spread his arms. The three of them fell, surrounded by coins and feathers. What was his subconscious trying to tell him? Did it have to do with the Purple Bouncer? With no answers forthcoming, Sam grabbed Willis's talon and the Tickler's arm.

"The eagles are waking! The eagles are waking!"

Blinking away the clouds, the frat party resolved around them. Handcuffed, but hand still vibrating, the Tickler scrambled out from under Sam. "Keep him away from me!"

Two angry police officers landed on the Tickler. The tickled girl stood, arms folded, looking like she wanted to be anywhere else. More students from the party gathered around.

Climbing to his feet, Sam walked back to the cruiser. Was this being a hero? Acting to save someone else from danger? He'd helped, even if he did get out of the car. It felt better than putting up a web site for ungrateful doctors.

It took a while to get the statements and details sorted out. A couple detectives came and interviewed all the witnesses. Sam kept his statement simple. He'd seen the officer in trouble and knew enough martial arts to take the young man to the ground. Even though they wrote it down, they obviously didn't believe him.

The detectives took the Tickler away, and Officer Johns came back to the cruiser. When he climbed into the driver's seat, he looked over at Sam. "That has to be the oddest thing I've ever seen. Thank you for keeping him from touching me."

"You're welcome. That kid might be difficult to keep in jail. I'd bet he can shatter the lock on a cell just like he did your night stick."

"Yeah. Good thing you were there. What did you do? It looked like you fell asleep." Officer Johns started the car and pulled away from the frat house.

Sam chuckled. "I did. The N stands for Narcolepsy."

Johns did a double-take and burst out laughing. Sam didn't mind, but one day he'd face a competent villain, like the Purple Bouncer.

5
The Minor Leagues

S am got the call at work. He'd picked up a pre-paid cell phone and routed it through an IP phone proxy so the police wouldn't be able to find him. He'd added a voice modulator too. The ring jolted Sam from sleep, where he'd been walking down a country road going nowhere, accompanied by a bouncing ball. Before answering, Sam slipped from the room divided into cubicles for the IT staff and into the stairwell at the hallway's end. "Narcolepsy here."

"This is dispatch. We have a man walking through walls. Responding units have requested special assistance."

"Where?"

"Five Points."

"Have an officer meet me at Panorama Park in fifteen minutes." Sam hung up and stepped back into the room, stopping at the cubicle across from his. "Hi, Mary. I have an emergency. If anyone wants me, I'll be back in a bit."

Before Mary could ask any questions, Sam slipped out, climbed the stairs to the back door, jogged to the parking lot, and drove away. Minutes later, with Sam in costume, he and Officer Johns screamed into Five Points with sirens blaring. "We caught the guy on camera here," Johns pointed to an ATM on Welton Street. "He just walked through the ATM, taking the money with him."

"He must have fine control, and if I can't touch him, it may be tricky."

Johns shrugged. "Can't do worse than us. He walked through our tasers, bullets, and cars."

Up ahead, four more police cruisers drove northeast at a walking pace with lights flashing. Others had blocked Welton so no other cars could approach. One man strolled on the sidewalk with a cloth grocery bag, ignoring the police.

A plan formed in Sam's mind, a perfectly pacifist plan. "Take me around the far side where he can't see."

Johns whipped the cruiser around the next corner and flipped on the siren to get cars out of the way. Moments later, he turned it all off again to disguise where Sam came from and cruised to a stop. Sam hopped out and walked down the sidewalk toward Welton. A light rail train rumbled past. A westerly spring breeze cooled the sun-warmed air. Shiny new stores and expensive apartments warred with old warehouses and rundown homes, with the new places winning. Across the street stood another bank with an ATM. Sam made for it, as if he needed cash, though his spandex would make that errand ridiculous.

He arrived as the man with the grocery bag slipped into the machine as if walking through a waterfall. Could this guy quantum-align atoms? Matter itself was mostly empty space. What a weird idea. Sam doubted this guy had any clue how he did it.

When Phase Boy re-emerged, stuffing cash into his sack, Sam stared. "Wow. Are you a superhero? How do you do that?"

The guy jumped. He appeared to be young and Hispanic, with intense eyes and thick, black hair. He gave Sam the once-over, frowning at the spandex. "I just want to go through, so I do."

Sam frowned. "Don't you have to wear spandex to be a hero?"

"Who are you?" Phase Boy asked.

Dismissing himself with a deprecating wave, Sam grinned and shrugged. "I'm a minor league hero, with a miniscule power. You really need to wear spandex, you know. It helps people understand what's going on." Sam, ATM card in hand, turned toward the machine. "Oh. Oh, well." With a weary sigh, he turned to walk away.

"Hold on," Phase Boy reached in and pulled a couple twenties from the bag. "Here, take these."

Returning his attention to Phase Boy, Sam reached out to take the bills. "Really? You don't want to keep all the money?"

"I don't keep any of the money. I give it all away," Phase Boy said. He reached in his bag and pulled out some more. "Here."

Blinking, Sam took the bills, considering what he could spend it on. Guilt bloomed in his chest. Even if this guy gave it to him, it would amount to stealing. "Wow, thanks!" He conjured a puzzled look and leaned closer. "Could you walk me through a wall?" Sam wondered how it would feel.

Phase Boy blinked. "Uh, maybe."

"Let's do it!" Sam reached out a hand.

"Um…I guess." He took Sam's hand and headed, not back to the ATM, but through the wall at the building's corner. When Sam's arm went into the stone, he almost pulled back. It worked! What happened if he let go now? He followed Phase Boy through. It felt like being in water, except it didn't part. It flowed through him, causing a mighty itch in his lungs and liver.

He couldn't see, which freaked him out. Phase-Boy could leave him in the wall! A shudder built in Sam, but he held it in, and held his breath. Cool, clear air encircled his hand again, and his forearm, but he still couldn't see. The darkness told his brain to sleep. His eyelids drooped, but Sam fought it as more of him emerged from the wall. He had to stay awake.

He lost the battle. Sam's eyes shut. He fell…

…And landed on softness—a car's seat, with Sam shotgun, for a change. Phase Boy drove as they headed out on the highway, bobble-head gopher on the dash and a purple garter hanging from the mirror. White lines flashed in the headlights, but they encountered no other cars. Beside the road, darkness held sway.

Phase Boy tried to slow down or turn, to no effect. Then he closed his eyes and concentrated, as if trying to sink through the car. It didn't work. "What have you done? Where the hell are we?"

Sam cocked his head. "Out on the open road, I'd say." Phase Boy glared, and Sam chuckled. "What? You don't like my power? I think it's kind of cool."

Letting go of the wheel, Phase Boy folded his arms. The car didn't care, moving down the road without swerving at all. "Why are you trying to stop me?"

"Well, you are a thief."

Phase Boy rolled his eyes and waved his arms. "You don't get it. These banks take all our money. They're insured. Their customers get their money back. I'm going to give..." He looked around for the bag. "Where's the money? People need it!"

Sam considered this Hispanic man, angry at the banks. Companies who put money ahead of people, who encouraged people to drowned in debt, deserved to be punished or changed in some way. Still, stealing was stealing. "You should reconsider your tactics, if you want to be Robin Hood. What you're doing just makes the police angry."

Before Phase Boy could answer, the gopher on the dash grew a policeman's hat and Sergeant Willis's head. It kept bobbling. "Hi, Kid. Looks like I'm back. I swear I didn't touch him, just the cuffs. Whoa, this is too bumpy."

"That wouldn't happen if you were a real dog. Come down here, Boy." Sam said.

Willis glared, but hopped down onto the seat, now a retriever with a policeman's head.

Sam couldn't resist. "Hey, Robin Hood, pet the dog." He held out his hand. "Shake, Willis."

The retriever raised a paw, which Sam took. Phase Boy laid a hand on the dog's neck and scratched. Willis groaned in pleasure, which turned to a growl.

Sam said, "Wake up, Boy! Wake us up!"

The dark night turned blue as the car vanished and they fell. They landed on the sidewalk, harder than they should have, scraping elbows and bashing knees. By the time Sam recovered, the police already had Phase Boy in handcuffs. Sam sat on the sidewalk and watched, wondering why the dude didn't just phase through the cuffs. Had he decided to turn himself in?

An officer gave him a hand up. A few minutes later, Sam rode back toward the park in the patrol car. Officer Johns shook his head. "We need more like you. How did you do that?"

Sam shrugged. "I chatted with him."

Johns laughed. At least Sam could amuse policemen.

At the park, he changed clothes and drove back to work, then stayed until after six before making his weary way home. The door unlocked as he approached, and when he walked in, he found Donelle lying on the couch, wearing his Sunday-go-to-meeting shirt and nothing else. A plastic platter on the coffee table held strawberries and blueberries, cheese and crackers. "My boss is representing today's guy and the frat boy. He's grateful."

Taking in her legs, the food, and what she'd said, Sam opened his mouth and didn't know what to comment on first. Being a hero had some benefits, and he'd succeeded tonight, protecting police officers of all people. He stepped around the table, sat down at her waist, and scooted back against her hips. Her warm body against him felt so good. He laid a hand on her thigh. He felt so guilty for his arousal. His actions had grown past his childhood shaming, but his subconscious had not. "I am grateful for you."

She ran a hand through his hair. "Should I feel guilty for seducing a good boy like you?"

"No. I wasn't a virgin. It's hard to go back. I…" The shame he'd endured for touching himself or looking at pictures welled up like black tar, threatening to engulf him. He resisted, telling himself to enjoy the attraction. His parents had misinformed and lied to him.

Donelle picked up a strawberry and stuffed it into his mouth. "Sometimes I want to smack your parents for all the shame they heaped on you."

Imitating her, Sam fed her a cheese cube, though she managed to suck on his finger in the process. They combined eating with foreplay.

A half hour later, Sam and Donelle stood naked in an empty bank lobby, front windows looking out at a high-rise across the street. There didn't seem to be any people around.

"This could get old," Donelle said, but she leapt into his arms, wrapping her legs around his waist.

Sam sat down in a side chair by a loan officer's desk. Voices reached them from around the office, approaching voices. None came closer than Sam's peripheral vision. He could hear them, though. "What's going on? Is that appropriate? Why are they here? I can do better than that."

Resting her forehead on his, Donelle scowled. "Old fast."

A purple ball bounced through the window, sending shattered glass through the lobby. Robin Hood followed, leaping through the window in green tights and tunic, complete with pointed hat and feather decoration. He shot out the security cameras with arrows, then put a series into the lock on the vault door. The shafts spun the combination wheel until the door swung open. Robin dashed in and came out carrying a couple dozen money bags and a computer.

The voices around the lobby still murmured about Sam and Donelle, so Sam shook his head. "Hey, Robin! Can you pop the dream bubble so we can wake up?"

Robin, looking a lot like Errol Flynn, only in real color, smiled. "Sure, Sam." He aimed and fired an arrow at nothing, somewhere Sam couldn't see.

With a pop, they woke on the couch. Sam breathed, trying to relax with Donelle resting atop him. Banks, money, and Robin Hood. "Are banks evil?"

Donelle frowned. "I think they can be both good and bad, like any human endeavor. They can protect people's money and give them loans for important things like cars and houses, but when they take people's houses, or teach and encourage us to get further and further in debt, that's a whole other thing."

That made sense. Just being a big company didn't make it evil, but any collection of humans could become evil or do evil. "Are people so oppressed that they want Robin Hood to rescue them?"

6
Perchance to Dream

Sam rode in the squad car again, late in the warm spring evening. That night, cruising the streets had been extra boring, without even a traffic ticket, and he didn't have Donelle to look forward to—she had a trial coming up, meaning she had to work eighteen-hour days.

The radio crackled and the dispatcher's monotone came over the airwaves. "Code 13, Fifteenth and Market. Respond code 9."

Officer Johns picked up his radio. "Car forty-seven responding code 9." He accelerated but hit neither lights nor siren.

"What's a code 13?" Sam asked. He'd studied the codes. They only used a dozen or so, but he'd never heard this one.

Johns laughed. "It's a costume clown, like you."

They drove downtown to where the streets ran at angles, along and away from the Platte River. At a German-themed bar, patrons ran out as Officer Johns pulled up. Light flashed inside.

Dashing in, Sam found wood décor, a bar running down the left side, and a bocce ball court dominating the room's center. There, a tall young man brought his hands together, shooting a light beam at a thick-set guy wearing a yellow spandex suit. Yellow ducked and dodged the beams, his feet a blur and his suit leaving a yellow streak behind him. The light beams blew up chairs and wood railings.

A waitress cowered on the floor by the concierge stand. Sam knelt beside her. "Who's the bad guy here?"

Wide-eyed, she glanced toward the combatants she couldn't see. "Umm…the guy in yellow is trying to help. The other guy got mad at someone he said cheated at bocce ball."

"How do you cheat at bocce ball?" Johns asked.

Sam turned to Officer Johns. "Get her out. I'll see if I can get behind mad laser guy."

Another laser beam set the wood railing on fire. Officer Johns shook his head. "This is nuts. Where are these spandex psychos coming from?" He clicked the mic on his collar. "Officer 519 on scene. Dispatch fire. Come on, ma'am. Let's get out of here." He held out a hand, which she took, relief showing on her face. He and the waitress ran out, bent over. Johns had a good point. These superpowers hadn't existed a decade ago. What could cause such absurd abilities?

With the laser beams heading toward the front, Sam resisted hurrying as he strode along the bar to the back. On impulse, he picked up what looked like two full beers from a table near the kitchen entrance before strolling around the corner onto the bocce ball court. Another man lay moaning against the wall with holes burned in his clothes.

"Hey, you look like you could use a beer." Sam held one out and took a drink from the other. He made a face at the taste. He hated wheat beer. He just hated beer.

Laser Guy turned and stepped toward Sam, wobbling. Yellow used the distraction to charge. He hit Laser Guy, knocking him into Sam. Beer drenched them as the mugs went flying. By reflex, Sam grabbed both of them to keep from falling. It didn't work. They went down in a pile, Sam on the bottom.

His head slammed into the wood floor. His ears rang in time with the pounding behind his eyes. "Not too bright…" Holding both men, Sam's eyes fluttered closed.

The stale beer smell followed them to a concession line in a fieldhouse. Five people stood in front of Sam, who couldn't focus his eyes, leaving the whole scene blurry.

Yellow hit Laser guy in the face. When Laser punched him back, the guy handing out beers shouted at them. "No rough-housing in the line!" For some reason, both costume clowns settled down. The counter-man poured beer, handed out pretzels, and took money, but the line didn't get any shorter.

Sam needed to get his beer and go. He had a task to do. What? Something important. The way the line never changed made Sam nervous. In dreams, that kind of weirdness was always a bad sign. The beer's smell combined with that of burned wood. Flames leaped out from the tunnel into the arena. Sam went to help, but the concession man waved him back. "You want beer? You stay in line."

Laser guy elbowed Yellow in the stomach when the beer guy looked away. Yellow smacked the back of Laser's head. Sam snickered.

The line of standing people morphed into a drive-through, and somebody handed Sam three beers and three pretzels through the window. The car moved on, turning and driving on its own. Sam didn't recognize the streets. A siren wailed, and Sam looked in the rearview mirror to find the lights, but he didn't see them.

"Where are we going?" Laser asked from the back seat.

"To work," Sam said, recognizing the sounds—the siren and squealing tires of an ambulance. The streets resolved to familiar ones, though the headstones of the cemetery loomed eerily overhead. The sky went from light to dark, but no stars came out.

A uniformed guy Sam didn't know popped into the passenger seat. He looked like an EMT. "What the hell? Where are we?"

"We're going to work." Why would they be going to work? It made no sense. He just couldn't think straight. There was something important about banks, money, and a purple ball. Or was it a purple Robin Hood?

A guy in a lavender tunic appeared, wearing plum leggings and a carrying fancy carbon fiber recurve bow, lilac colored, of course. He shot an arrow at a purple ball that bounced by. An arrow would be bad for a rubber ball. Some kid would be upset. That made no sense. How could a dream be so confusing? It was like he got hit on the head or something.

The sirens stopped. The ambulance they rode in had arrived at the hospital. Sam got out and stepped directly into the silent, basement IT offices. The aromas of antiseptic and microwave popcorn filled the room in a nauseating blend. Announcements came over the intercom. Doctors and nurses spoke to each other in a wordless drone, like the adults in a Charlie Brown Special, but the IT offices remained still as the grave. Sam sat at his desk, thinking he should build a new server. None of this made sense, but he had to do something. His boss would be angry again. Maybe caffeine would help.

"Oh, yeah, I am at work," the EMT said. Where had he come from? Sam jumped up and knocked his pens on the floor. When he bent to pick them up, he bumped the cubical wall. It crashed to the ground, knocking the next one over too. Now the boss would really be mad.

The EMT walked out and up the stairs.

"Where are we?" Yellow asked, popping in beside the desk along with Laser Guy.

Sam jumped. Why didn't dream feet make noise?

"What the hell is going on? Why am I not drunk?" Laser asked.

Sam didn't know, although he had a powerful feeling he was forgetting something, something important. Robin Hood. It had to do with Robin Hood, or flying monkeys, or banks. He'd better hurry up and . . .and do what?

A woman in scrubs appeared, hands on hips. She glared at Laser Guy like it was all his fault. Maybe it was. "What the hell am I doing in IT?"

~~~~

Dr. Gillian Giles stepped over to the ER nurse's station and yawned. She hated night shifts. That's what nurses and interns were for, but three ER providers had gone down with influenza, and she had done an ER residency before becoming intrigued with sleep disorders. It had been a quiet night, so far.

The radio crackled, dispatch reporting a bar fight and superheroes. Gillian sighed. There would be civilian casualties. Gillian got the teams ready, waiting at the door for the ambulances.

Sirens presaged their arrival, but only three came in. The first had a guy in ordinary clothes, unconscious, handcuffed to his gurney, and accompanied by a police officer. "This is the guy who caused all the issues. He shoots lasers or something." Before he could say more, the orderlies whisked the patient-prisoner away to start their exam.

The second ambulance rolled up, but the EMT didn't jump out. The nurses opened the doors and found the EMT slumped over a guy in dark spandex. A nurse jumped up and shook the EMT. "Are you...oooh." She collapsed onto the EMT.

What the hell? "Ignore them. Get the gurney!" Gillian shouted.

Two orderlies leaped forward and dragged the gurney off the ambulance and into the ER. The EMT and nurse slithered to the ambulance floor. A third ambulance rolled up. What would come on that one? She decided to follow the second gurney in anyway.

They'd taken the guy in dark spandex to Bay Two, divided by curtains from one and three. As Gillian walked up, a nurse leaned over the gray guy and tapped his shoulder—the correct first step, see if he's conscious. "Are you awake? Can you hear me? Pleee..." Her voice trailed away and she collapsed down on spandex guy.

Another nurse dashed over. "Claire! What's wrong?"

"No!" Gillian shouted, but not before the second nurse tried to wake Claire. The second nurse blinked and slid to the floor against Claire's legs. Her arm fell under the curtain and brushed a resident giving care instructions to a mom and a kid who'd gotten sixteen stitches skateboarding through the cemetery. The resident looked down, yawned, and flopped across the boy.

The mom, puzzled, shook the doctor. "Are you okay?" She laid a hand on her son's shoulder and collapsed across him next to the resident. Her foot hit the IV pole, knocking it into the next curtain.

An orderly mopping out that bay and getting it ready for the next patient stepped on the pole and fell backward. He grabbed the curtain for support and went down. His back came to rest against the mom's legs, and his head nodded forward.

A nurse from around the corner, who hadn't seen all the rest, ran toward the orderly. Gillian screamed. "Everyone, stop! No one touch anyone!" Gillian looked around the suddenly silent ER. Two nurses had a gurney with a guy in yellow spandex by the door. Outside, some people pulled the original EMT and nurse out of the second ambulance. That mattered, but first she needed to get the ER in order. "Get away from bays two, three, and four. No one goes near them without my express permission. Put that yellow guy, the nurse, and EMT in six, seven and eight. If they aren't bleeding, leave them alone. Move!"

While the staff ran to obey her, moving a couple patients in the process, Gillian considered. Down three nurses and a resident, how much more could she lose and keep the ER open?

The charge nurse walked over. "What the hell?"

Gillian shook her head. "I don't know. See if you can get a couple more nurses in here while I figure this out." She turned in a circle, spying three more residents. She could spare one. "Doctor Kahtri, I need you. Come."

Without waiting, she went over to Bay 2 and leaned close to the man in gray spandex. He had a big N on his chest. What was the deal with these spandex costumes anyway? She spotted a little blood in his hair, so he might have a brain injury. His respiration rate came in at fifteen, so just fine. She counted throbs in his neck to get a pulse. Giving him a quick visual scan, she stopped on his eyes—which showed rapid movement beneath the lids. REM sleep? Why would he be in REM sleep?

Dr. Kahtri came up behind her but didn't speak. She appreciated a resident who could pay attention. Gillian straightened up. Her experiment needed to start at the other end. Walking down to Bay 8, she found the ER Nurse that had mounted the ambulance. "Doctor Kahtri, examine her, please."

He gave Gillian a doubletake, swallowed hard, and bent close. Rolling her eyes, Gillian gave him a light slap on the back of his head. "A real examination. Pulse, respiration, whatever you deem appropriate."

"But..." He gestured toward Bay 2.

"This is an experimental diagnosis. Together we will find out what is wrong, and I will fix it." Gillian pointed at the nurse in scrubs lying on the bed.

After hesitating, Dr. Kahtri swallowed hard and took the nurse's pulse. He blinked in surprise when he didn't fall asleep. He went on, taking her blood pressure, respiration, and even checking her pupillary reactions. When he finished, he straightened up, puzzled. Deciding, he leaned down and shook the nurse's shoulder. "Can you hear me? Wake up." When the woman didn't move, Dr. Kahtri looked at Dr. Giles. "Um..."

Gillian scowled and looked at the nurse's eyes. They too showed REM. "What did your diagnosis find?"

"I think she's asleep, but I can't wake her up."

Turning, Gillian headed toward Bay 2. "I concur. Time for the next step." With Dr. Kahtri following like a puppy, Gillian stopped at the bed's foot. The effect appeared to be touch related, but did it only work with body parts? "Grab an IV pole and see if you can push Nurse Claire away from our costumed insomnia cure." If Kahtri stayed awake, they'd be able to get the others to beds at least, and with care, Mr. Insomnia Cure too.

"I need to get on a maternity rotation," Dr. Kahtri muttered as he walked away. Gillian hid her smile. Returning with a shorter, bed-mounted pole, Kahtri looked at Nurse Claire and knew Gillian would sacrifice him, or at least put him to sleep, to find out. With a sigh, he used the pole to slide Nurse Claire off Insomnia Cure and onto her friend.

Dr. Kahtri remained standing.

~~~~

Donelle paced. The hospital waiting room had semi-comfortable chairs and the antiseptic odor of all hospitals. When Sam hadn't answered her texts, at first, she thought he'd been busy, maybe out fighting bad guys. After three days, she got worried, but she'd been working her ass off and hadn't had time to go by his apartment.

When the trial started, her evenings freed up. She'd called and texted several times with no answer, and worry clouded her mind. The apartment let her in, and the rotting food stink assaulted her. The unmade bed she expected. However, when she tracked down the half-eaten burrito on the kitchen counter, she knew Sam had been hurt. He might have left the food there a few hours, but not days.

Distracted, and wondering what to do next, Donelle cleaned up the mess, all the way to taking the garbage over to the chute. After thinking for a bit, she called a friend at the police department while logging on to the court records to see arrests the night Sam had gone missing. Between those two sources, she'd located Sam at Lutheran Hospital. Now she had to convince the staff she knew how to help. A doctor walked in carrying a tablet, and Donelle turned toward her. Her name tag read, "Dr. Giles."

"Hello, Miss. Who are you?"

"I'm..." Did they know his name? He didn't carry ID as Narcolepsy. "I'm Narcolepsy's friend. I think I can help."

Dr. Giles' eyes narrowed. "You aren't a relative? Then I can't discuss his condition."

Scowling, Donelle paced again, thinking. "You don't have to tell me. I'll tell you. He's just sleeping. More, I can wake him up, along with..." Considering the emergency room, she laughed. "How many people have fallen asleep by touching him?"

"Um, a few," Dr. Giles said.

Donelle's smile got even wider. "And you can't wake them. I can wake them all."

The doctor pursed his lips. "All of them?" She gestured for Donelle to follow.

"Of course." Her mother's voice told her she couldn't do it, which let her understand Sam's mother in his dreams a little. Sam and the others had been asleep so long. Could they come back? Would Sam be able to bring them back? She followed the doctor down the hall to a ward where the rooms looked like they belonged in a luxury hotel rather than a hospital.

Before going into Sam's room, Dr. Giles stopped. "Tell us who he is, so we can get his medical records."

Donelle considered it. Did a secret identity help? What could his enemies do if they knew? No one could answer that, unless they could predict the future. She could imagine bad scenarios both ways. This current situation being one against. "The secret is not mine to keep or give. All I need is to join him for a bit."

Dr. Giles put hands on hips and scowled. "What? And use up another one of my beds?"

"I'll wake him up." The more she said it, the more flaws she saw in her assertion, and the more she doubted. She didn't know why he hadn't woken up on his own.

Dr. Giles sighed. "Oh, all right." She gestured to the second room down. "Are you sure you won't tell us who he is?"

A nurse walking by stopped and looked in the room. "Him? That's Sam from IT. He installed our new server last year."

Face getting red, Dr. Giles rounded on her nurse. "And you didn't deign to…you've been on vacation." She folded her hands over her face. "Sorry and thank you. Sam from IT." She turned back to Donelle, raising an eyebrow.

Donelle rolled her eyes. "Yes, he's Sam Neufeld from IT. May I try now?"

Holding up one hand, Dr. Giles opened his health record on her tablet. "He has narcolepsy. Of course he does. And the meds don't work. Of course they don't." She looked up and sighed. "I can spare another bed. Go on."

She'd done it now. Donelle walked in. When she saw Sam lying there, she wanted to stroke his hair and kiss his lips. She resisted. Instead, she shoved him over a little through the sheet and almost fell asleep. She crawled in beside him and laid an arm and a leg across his body, snuggling close. Her eyes drooped and she drifted downward. "I'm coming, Sam."

The cushy sleep room dissolved into one with bare concrete walls. It looked a little like the hospital after a fire. It smelled different, and silence invaded like an enemy.

"Whoa. Who are you, hot stuff?"

Donelle turned to find a tall man she didn't know ogling her. Looking down, she found herself naked.

A thicker man with blond hair walked up and slapped the first man. A fight broke out, but it had an old air, like they'd been doing it so long they didn't care but didn't know how to walk away.

"Sam! Where are you?"

Peering around the corner, Sam looked puzzled. "What?"

"Get the fuck over here and give me some clothes!" Donelle said.

As he walked closer, the scene changed, becoming a rocky mountain slope with fragrant firs, sparse grass, and sharp granite boulders. Donelle got jeans and a flannel shirt. Three frightened nurses peered around trees or boulders. A teenage boy ran out and scrambled up a boulder. A woman followed, scowling. "Jason! Get down from there right now."

The boy ignored her. Another nurse joined the first three.

Donelle beckoned them. "Come on out. It's time for a camp fire."

As night fell, Sam walked over, trying to put his arms around her. When he got near, Donelle stopped him with a hand while the other two men laughed. "Oh, no, big fella. You have more important duties." She slapped him. "Grab everyone and wake us up!"

"Wha…oh, wake up!" Sam slapped his forehead, walked over to the bonfire, and sat on a log. "We need the other guys, though."

"What other guys?" Donelle asked.

"I don't know, just four guys."

"I'll go find them," a nurse said. Waving her flashlight back and forth, she strode off into the mountain night. It grew cold.

A few minutes later, as the waiting grew strained, the nurse came back leading the men.

Reaching out to the guy in yellow sitting on his other side, Sam said, "Everyone, hold hands." Donelle found the guy who'd ogled her on her right side. Somehow, he made holding hands creepy. When she looked, the mom, the kid, four nurses, two other guys in scrubs, and one EMT, plus the guy in yellow, sat on logs holding hands.

Sam still looked confused, so Donelle whispered to him. "Just wake us up."

"But I have to get to the bank. Robin Hood wants to perforate the purple ball. We have to stop them foreclosing, or a bank robbery, or something."

Nodding, Donelle squeezed his hand. "Rob from the rich and give to themselves, since they're poor. All we have to do is…" She paused and shouted. "Wake up!"

When Sam, in the real hospital bed, jumped, Donelle opened her eyes on the hospital room. Out in the corridor, a commotion erupted.

7
The Great Plains

Looking out the window at the endless flat land, miles and miles of wheat fields and pastures broken only by giant windmills, Jenna yawned. The four days with Noah's family had been enlightening, even though they thought she was his girlfriend. They had clippings of his robberies up on their fridge, and he'd given thousands in cash.

Jenna spoke up to keep herself awake. "Your family is supportive of your career choice."

Noah, who'd been dozing in the passenger seat, startled awake. "What? Oh, yes. I grew up on stories of how Jessie James and Pretty Boy Floyd stuck it to the man and helped the poor."

Laughing, Jenna shook her head. "I don't think we, or they, are quite so innocent."

That got a shrug from Noah. "Could be, but if the people protect us, it doesn't matter, does it?"

The man had a point. Jenna wondered what the people did with the jewelry from the mansions. It could get them arrested, but they'd been warned. Hopefully, they'd just keep them.

The conversation died, and twenty minutes later, still watching the Interstate stretching out before her. "Kansas is boring. How do you stand it?"

He laughed. "You're looking in the wrong place." He leaned forward, peering out the windshield and both sides. "Look there, on the horizon."

To the southwest, purple clouds stained the sky. The sun shone down, painting the cloud tops white and creating lighter rays angling to the ground. Lightning flashed, strobing through the daylight. To Jenna, storms had always rolled over and past them, with weather channels on TV and Internet the only warning. She stared at this high, powerful storm on the horizon.

"Um, you're drifting," Noah said.

With an adrenalin jolt, Jenna jerked the car off the shoulder. She drove for a bit, catching her breath. "That might be worth looking at."

Two hours later, they pulled into a gas station in Burlington, Colorado. Jenna stalked toward the door, wishing she could make someone bleed, the way she'd bled at her father's hands. Instead, she picked up a floppy hat and put it on as she walked into the clean, air-conditioned store. Her power worked on live video, but not on recordings, as near as she could tell. Then again, most people never recorded her at all. Sometimes she hated her power, wishing she'd gotten one like Noah instead.

Using what she had to cause mayhem, Jenna walked behind the counter and stood beside the cash register. When the man opened the register drawer with a chime, she reached in and took cash. She gathered all the tens and twenties and walked out with drinks and snacks as well. Behind her, the cashier stared in confusion at the empty bill slots.

Noah had finished filling the tank, so they drove away, Jenna counting the cash in the passenger seat. Noah shook his head. "How much does an island cost?" He paused. "How much before they can't bother us?"

Jenna looked askance at her partner. "When we get tired of stealing and killing, we can buy however much we can afford. Maybe we can buy lovers. Right now, it's too much fun."

"You are one sick individual," Noah said.

"Hey, you're the one who likes smashing things." They drove on another mile or two before Jenna spoke again. "We could just try to take over the world. Then no one would bother us."

Noah laughed. "Sure they would. There'd be armies and rebellions and heroes and all sorts of things to deal with."

"Good point. Hmm. Let's do that again, what we did at the gas station. This time at a gun store. I need a weapon."

"Sure."

Silence descended, and Noah turned on the radio searching among gospel and country stations. Jenna thought back to her childhood, feeling again her father's white-hot anger, feeling his hand impact her face, her arms, her back. She'd cultivated the ability to hide. Her older brother tried to stand up to him and got beaten down, so he looked for someone weaker to beat himself. As a teen, he, not her father, had come in to rape her. He'd also been the first person she ever killed. Her father had taken the fall for it.

~~~~

An hour later, Noah pulled off the Interstate and headed into Limon. "There has to be a gun shop around here somewhere."

It took a while, but eventually he found the Big R sporting goods store. A strong wind blew in from the west, bringing the stench of manure riding on the dust. Jenna grabbed her big purse and led the way in, wearing her floppy hat and calming her breathing so others wouldn't notice her. They walked past the fishing gear and hunting outfits to get to the firearms.

The man behind the counter had a military-looking rifle out to show to a young man wearing jeans and a dirty plaid shirt. "This rifle, with the bump stock and sixty round clips, lets you shoot five or six deer very quickly. There will be so many bullets in the air, nothing can survive. Works on trespassers and immigrants too."

Jenna shook her head as she stepped up beside the man buying the weapon. These guys made her look like Mary Poppins. First, she stole the guy's wallet. Then she grabbed the bump stock and put a cheap flashlight in its place. She hid the offending add-on amid the hunting blinds.

When she got back, she looked through the cases. There, with all the other handguns, she located a six-hundred-dollar Smith & Wesson 9-millimeter. Jenna leaned close to Noah. "Ask to see a reasonably priced handgun."

She slipped around behind the counter and grabbed three boxes of 9-millimeter rounds, the most expensive she saw. When the deer-slaughterer finished his purchase, Noah asked to see the weapons. The employee unlocked the door and slid it back, and Jenna reached in, grabbing the gun she wanted. Sometimes it all seemed too easy.

On the way out, she swapped one guy's shotgun shells for fishing lures, grabbed a wad of cash from a register, and took a telescopic sight from a guy walking out, giving him the shotgun shells instead.

As they drove out of the parking lot, Noah shook his head. "On the way to that private island nation of ours, lets cause some havoc."

8
Beds and Feds

The commotion in the corridor grew louder as Sam tried to place the hospital room. He groaned. What a long, weird dream. Why had he not woken up sooner? He'd forgotten to try to wake up. How long had it been? Blinking as he looked around, he found a soft bed, softer pillows, a stylish comforter, dresser, television, and carpeting. Incongruous with the décor, a panel on the wall held ports for oxygen, network connections and more. It smelled like antiseptic, in other words, work. Then it hit him; the sleep lab! Why was he in the sleep lab?

Donelle moved beside him, stretching and leaning over to kiss him. "Hello, Rip Van Winkle. Welcome back."

For a little, they both ignored the noises in the corridor. Sam blinked, trying to recall how he'd gotten here. "What happened? I remember offering someone a beer." Who? Strange flashes returned—light beams and a yellow blur. What had he been doing? What happened to the two bickering guys from the dream?

A doctor stepped over to shine a light in his eyes and take his pulse. "How are you feeling? You had a concussion, but that doesn't account for your long nap here."

Sam stared, mouth open. How did he feel? His limbs didn't want to move, one leg tingling as it recovered. His fingers felt thick. Concussion? His head didn't hurt. "Like waking up after sleeping too long. Considering I can't sleep at night, that's not bad."

The doctor nodded and typed on her tablet. "We'll get you up soon. First, I'd like…"

Someone shouted, "Doctor! They woke up." A hundred footfalls echoed through the ward. Someone else said, "What the hell happened?" Twenty people talked at once so Sam couldn't hear the words, as waking patients and their loved ones poured into the hallway.

Two men yelled at each other. When a laser beam flashed past the door, Sam leaped from the bed. His head pounded, but he gritted his teeth and went out into the crowd. The nurses and EMTs from the dream all shrank away, avoiding his touch. They pulled their loved ones back too. A small fire smoldered in an oil painting of puppies hanging in the corridor.

Sam flattened himself against the wall to dodge another blast. "All right, you morons, stop it!" He pushed past three people to the next room.

A thrown pillow from Yellow burst asunder when Laser blasted it. Feathers rained down. Using the distraction, Yellow leaped at Laser, crashing them both into a chair, which knocked over the bedside table and tangled tubing for an IV.

"Do I have to take you back into my dream?" Sam sounded like his mother.

Sudden silence descended on the scene. Everyone in the hall stopped with gasps and exclamations. "I liked his dreams," a teen said.

Both men froze. "Uh...no." Yellow Blur said.

Sam stood, hands on hips, glaring and not knowing what to do next. The bystanders pressed closer to get a look at who'd been fighting, as they realized Sam hadn't been threatening them with the dream. They all spoke at once, jostling forward. Some patted Sam on the back. The kid who wanted to dream again looked disappointed, though his mother cuffed him. Donelle and Dr. Giles came out to observe the confrontation.

Three hospital security guards pushed through the crowd. Sam raised a hand to stop them. "These two will go along peacefully. Won't you?"

"Yes, sir," Laser Guy said.

"Excellent," a new voice said. Two men in suits pushed through the crowd, drawing angry retorts. The suits flashed badges. "Let us through. Out of the way." The crowd in the hall didn't appear eager to assist, making these two newcomers twist, turn, and slide through. "Important business. Make way, please. People, we have government business!"

When they made it through the patients, visitors, nurses, EMTs, orderlies, providers, janitors, and security people, they came face to face with Donelle and Dr. Giles, both glaring.

The two feds had the same haircut, the same shades, and even stood the same height. It reminded Sam of the Cat in the Hat, only suits instead of things. Suit One looked past the women to Yellow and Laser. "We have an offer for you two."

Behind the suits, the kid crowded in, followed by the nurses and the other dreamers. "Hey! What deal are you talking about? We like Sean and want to keep him."

"Yeah," Sean said. "I'm just your friendly neighborhood Yellow Blur."

Suit One smiled. "You should hear us out first. We're offering you an opportunity to use your special powers to serve your country."

Laser stepped forward. "I'm interested. The marines washed me out two years ago."

"You're mean, too," the kid said, folding his arms. Donelle tried to hide her smile.

"I would rather be a local Five Points hero. I even have a badge." Sean felt where his pockets would be if he'd been wearing pants, then searched the little nightstand. He came up with an unofficial-looking stamped-brass badge.

Sam leaned close. The badge said, "Friendly Neighborhood Yellow Blur." Sam rubbed his head, which throbbed. "I should get one of these."

"I'll hook you up with the guy who made that for me. I did have to buy five." Sean handed it to Sam for a better look.

Turning the fake badge over in his hand, Sam cocked his head. "I wonder if you could put a locator chip in this?" Maybe he could have sticky locator chips to put on cars or bad guys too. "There might be other tech we could use. Maybe we could work together to figure it out."

"I like it." He cuffed Sam's shoulder. "Hey, sorry for knocking you out, man."

"It could happen to anybody. Well, maybe not me. We should work together…"

"I think they have misconstrued our offer," Suit Two said.

Suit One nodded. "A misapprehension indeed." He raised a hand for silence, but no one paid attention. "Ahem. You gentlemen are under the delusion that we offered you a choice."

"What?" Sam and Donelle said together. The onlookers grew restless, crowding the feds.

Donelle still barring the door, held out a hand. "Let's see the arrest warrant."

Suit Two laughed. "We don't need a warrant. The Favored Persons Act gives us—"

Suit One raised a hand to stop him and loomed over Donelle. "There are two ways this happens. One, you come with us now, or two, you get arrested, tried, and convicted of inciting a riot plus assault and battery. When sentenced, it will be to federal prison, where you will work with us, regardless."

Donelle pulled out her phone and texted someone. "I represent their attorney. There have been no federal crimes here. These men are waiting for the Denver police."

Suit One shrugged, with an added smirk. "Have it your way. We'll get them in the end." He reached into his briefcase and pulled out what looked like a hundred-page document. "They need to fill out these." He handed the papers to Donelle.

Her attention grew sharper than Laser Guy's beams as she skimmed the opening pages to get to the meat. Donelle moved through the provisos and provisions with alacrity, but the document seemed to grow with each sheet she flipped over.

The natives grew restless until Suit One, thinking Donelle distracted, tried to slip past. Donelle stuck out an arm to block the door. "What's this shit about a 'Favored Persons Act'?"

A commotion broke out in the hall. Two men in uniforms pushed through the crowd, drawing angry retorts. They flashed badges. "Let us through. Out of the way." The crowd in the hall didn't appear eager to assist, making these two newcomers twist, turn, and slide through. "Police business. Make way, please. People, we have police business!"

The officers stopped behind the two suits. One pointed at Laser and Yellow. "We have arrest warrants for you and you."

"That was fast," Sam said.

Yellow Blur looked at the crowd in the corridor, then over at the suits and police officers. "Um, I think I choose door number one." He pointed at the Suits as he turned to Donelle. "Should I sign…?"

Donelle no longer had the document in her hands. Instead, she gave Sean her business card. "I wouldn't, no, but you may not have much choice. Call me if you can. You too." She gave a second card to Laser.

Looking around the room, Sam didn't see many options besides attacking the suits. Even if Donelle's bosses had been here, he doubted they could stop these guys. Besides, he'd just woken up from days in a dream. He didn't want to go back under again. Although, one thing puzzled him. "Why aren't you taking me?"

Suit One gave him half a smile. "We think you're more useful catching these guys for us." He fished in his jacket and came up his own business card, which he handed to Sam. "Call us if you need a job."

Sam didn't know how to respond, so he took the card, which said Agent Jason Jones, Homeland Security.

A couple hours later, Sam led Donelle into his little apartment. After the feds left with Yellow and Laser, the doctors wanted to poke and prod Sam, to make sure he could be discharged. The sleep doctor, Dr. Giles, asked him question after question about his sleep patterns and how he could stay asleep so long.

Donelle, buried in her phone, muttered to herself. "LexisNexis, show me your stuff. Why am I a favored person? Maybe I'm not favored, because you aren't helping." As soon as they walked in the door, she said, "I can't find this Favored Persons Act. I need your computer." From her bag, she pulled the stack of papers Suit One had given her. "There's some weird wording in this mess."

"You stole that? Good work." Sam opened his laptop on the coffee table and logged in for her. "Welcome home, Sam. How are you feeling, Sam? I'm doing fine, but I don't like losing four days." Getting up again, he went to the fridge to see if he had any food. He hadn't eaten in forever. The fuzzy leftovers tempted him.

"I can take you back," Donelle said, without looking up.

With Donelle bent over the laptop and talking to herself, Sam called a sandwich shop to deliver a couple hoagies, with chips and drinks. While waiting, he played word-puzzle games on his phone. He should have been checking his work emails, but didn't feel like it.

When the food arrived, Donelle sat up and closed the laptop. "I can't find it. There is nothing in LexisNexis, meaning lawyers know nothing about it." She took a long drink of her soda. "Oh, that's good. Thank you."

Turning his sandwich in his hands, Sam wondered how a law letting the feds take people away could avoid lawyers' attention, except they hadn't been arrested. Suit one and Suit Two hadn't given them a choice, though. "What if it's not criminal law?"

Donelle stopped with a barbeque chip halfway to her mouth. "Not criminal…the Congressional Record!" She ate the chip, wiped her fingers, and leaned forward to open the laptop again. It took her half an hour more, with Sam watching and making suggestions, to find the bill. Once she'd read it, she leaned back and rubbed her neck. "Very odd."

Sam read a section aloud. "We are commanded by our sacred duties to conclude that forthcoming national safekeeping proceedings and clandestine conflicts will hinge on registering specialized skills and enrolling the succor of those regarded as localized favored persons." Sam took a deep breath and recovered for a moment. "What the hell?"

Donelle laughed but grew serious right away. "I have to go through it again, but as near as I can tell, it's a draft notice for people with extraordinary abilities. It even allows the use of force for resisters or draft dodgers."

"So, they could just take me away?"

After taking another long drink, Donelle laid a hand on his neck and pulled him close. She leaned her forehead against his. "Not if I can help it. They did say they liked you out here. I suspect they can't think of a use for your talent."

Sam imagined being in an army with the Tickler, Yellow Blur, and Laser Guy. Maybe Metallo and Scream, plus the Purple Bouncer too. "Me, in an army." He chuckled. "Surrender, or I'll fall asleep!"

"You've done well so far, but teamwork *might* not be your biggest asset." Donelle kissed him.

When she came up for air, Sam asked the next question. "If they are making a clandestine fighting unit, what happens to the people, like Laser Guy, who prove too intractable to be useful?"

"Nothing good." Donelle rubbed her eyes. "The government, without admitting it to its citizens, is creating a superpowered combat and espionage unit. Why? Maybe it doesn't matter. Even with the best intentions, it could be used for evil. A lot depends on the available powers."

Neither said a word for a while. If he had a more orthodox power, Sam would be... He shivered, thankful for being so strange, and pulled out the Suit One's business card. "Homeland Security, Research and Investigation Department. Interesting. Not recruitment."

With a sigh, Donelle leaned against him, resting her head on his shoulder. "I want to forget all this for a while." She rose and offered a hand. "Let's cuddle."

"Ah, to cuddle, perchance to dream."

Donelle led him to the bed and they laid down together—Sam on his back, and Donelle on her side, head on his shoulder and one leg over him. He treasured her body against his. He wanted to jump her bones, but he'd settle for this. Soon he and Donelle cavorted with some dragons on puffy cloud—a cotton candy cloud.

Later, while Donelle slept, Sam sat in bed with his laptop researching the Purple Bouncer. After New York, he'd hit Chicago, robbing an armored car followed by smashing some of the biggest mansions in the city. In each case, at least some of the money had been given to people who gathered to watch. That continued as they moved south, robbing small-town branches of big banks. There weren't any small banks anymore. At the third one, the FBI had setup shop waiting for him, not that it had mattered much. Then, after St. Louis and a couple banks and mansions, the Purple Bouncer had vanished. He hadn't struck since.

"He's coming here," Sam said. He could feel it in his bones.

9
Interview

"Sam! Wake up!" His boss's voice echoed across the dream landscape. He jumped. The basement office cubicle resolved around him. Before dozing off, he'd been trying to figure out these stupid hard junctions on some server folders. Who had made this crap? "Huh? What?"

Sam's boss shook his head and pointed to the conference room. "There's a reporter here to see you."

"Me? Why?" His boss had already walked on.

Sam rubbed his eyes and followed his boss to the little conference room in the corner. A young woman wearing a red suit sat at the round table. She had a tablet with a microphone plugged in. When Sam stopped in the door, she rose and gave him a movie-star smile. "Hi, I'm Sarah Singleton from Westword. Are you Narcolepsy?"

Sighing, Sam stepped into the room and sat down, though it surprised him a little, given Sarah's looks, that no TV station had poached her from that small-time newspaper. Another thought seeped into his brain; he wanted to help her. "Me? I'm just a system administrator."

"What is your power, anyway? The reports from the bar fight have you giving a guy a beer, and next thing you three are in the hospital."

That offered Sam a topic to distract her, still harboring a vain hope to preserve his secret identity. "That does about cover it. One guy could shoot lasers from his hands. He seemed upset, so I gave him a beer, or tried to. The other guy knocked us both down. An odd thing happened when we woke up though. A couple of federal agents showed up and took the other two guys away."

Sarah looked puzzled. "Why? A bar fight is not a federal offense."

He had her right where he wanted, now. Sam shrugged. "Don't know. They mentioned a Favored Persons Act."

"What? What's that?"

Sam shrugged again. "Don't ask me. I'm a system admin."

Looking at her tablet, Sarah typed a bit. "I guess I'll have to find out. I, um…" Sam had thrown her off her game. She looked at her notes, took a deep breath and launched. "What most readers want to know is where are all these super powers are coming from?"

Now she'd surprised him. What a fabulous question. Sam stared and stammered. "I…well…wow." How could he not have asked this question? Where did Metallo and Scream come from? The Purple Bouncer? Tickler and Laser Guy, all at once? What could have caused it?

Sarah deflated, slumping in her chair. "This is the first time I've found someone with a power. I thought you might know."

"Maybe I should. Then again, what I do isn't even good enough for the feds to be interested in me. More of a novelty." Their snub hurt, in an odd way. He didn't want to join their secret cadre, but he had subdued a thief and four other guys with strange powers.

"What is your power?" Sarah had her game and her smile back. Again, Sam wanted to cooperate and give her what she wanted.

He chuckled. "I fall asleep."

"That's not a power!"

Sam shrugged. He wanted to take Sarah into his dreams, but somehow, he didn't think Donelle would like that. Not one bit. "Well, you would go to sleep too. It makes people much easier for the police to capture, and that doesn't even count the haunted forest or the empty road."

"That makes no sense."

"I could have mentioned the dragons or the six-foot bobble-head gopher with a policeman's hat. You wanted to know about my power."

With a head shake, Sarah rose to leave. "You don't have to make fun of me."

Sam got to his feet, feeling bad that he'd told her the truth without explaining. "I was not making fun of you. It's all true…" Sam could see she didn't believe him. Time to cut his losses. "While I give you permission to talk about Narcolepsy, don't use my name, or even say I work at this hospital."

Sarah pursed her lips. "I agree. You aren't interesting enough. Although, you might get some laughs." She paused again and shook her head. "I wish you knew what had caused all these super powers. Thank you for your time." Putting away her microphone, she offered her hand.

Sam shook it and cocked his head. "Have you considered your own superpower?"

"What? What do you mean?" She blushed. She did know.

"Getting people to cooperate with you. If I find out where our powers came from, I'll let you know."

Sarah left a card, and Sam wondered if he could trust her. He'd find out when her story came out. That she could find him did not bode well. Someone in this hospital had violated HIPAA regulations and told on him. Sam's boss came to mind.

It didn't matter, though. Sam had to work late, staying to make up for sleeping during the day. If only he could sleep at night.

Three days later, the new Westword came out. Sam and Donelle went to the Blue Bonnet restaurant on South Broadway to celebrate a court victory for her law firm where their client had been sued for using an offensive paint color on their store. The firm gave Donelle a bonus for getting all the documents and pleadings ready for trial.

On the way in, leaning into a brisk south wind as the sun set behind the mountains, they found the new Westword on the rack inside the door. Sam picked one up. The front-page cartoon showed a guy in spandex with a cape, standing arms akimbo.

Donelle laughed. "Are you trying to pick up some hot young chick?"

"Um…no." The personals in the back had a racy reputation. You could find hookups there, and hookers too. "I thought perhaps Ms. Singleton's article might be here."

Taking the paper as they walked to a table, Donelle sniffed. "We have to at least *look* at the ads." She flipped it open to the back and spent the next ten minutes teasing him about the male enhancement opportunities and maybe getting laid if he answered a woman seeking companionship. Sam wanted to go get another copy for himself.

After they ordered burritos smothered with pork green chili, Sam managed to get the paper back from her. The puerile picture on the cover made him think Sarah had gotten her article done. Seven pages in, another drawing showed the same caped guy flying, arms out, even though the title said, "Government Hoarding Super Powers."

"I could have demonstrated my powers for young Sarah Singleton." Sam continued reading the article. She had located the Favored Persons Act, and it said just what they thought. The feds could abscond with any super-powered person. True to her word, she did not mention his name or much he'd said, but, to demonstrate that super-powered people held jobs, had families, and lived in the community, she mentioned he worked in IT in the medical field. "Damn. I think my secret identity will be going down the drain." He turned the paper around and pointed to the spot.

Donelle frowned. "With the ability to locate people on the Internet, I suspect you're right. What then?"

Sam hadn't considered it much. In the comics, bad guys would threaten Donelle so he could rescue her. They might ambush him at his apartment or at work. That would get him fired. "I need to reduce my personal online presence, unlist my phone, lock my credit report, etc. I might even create an online presence for Narcolepsy, with misleading information."

"What about me?"

Telling her the truth might…he had to, though, unless he retired as a superhero. Did superheroes retire? Did they have a pension plan? Medical benefits? What about nursing homes?

"Well, dating a superhero can be rough. I'll always be breaking dates and dashing off to fight villains, not to mention falling asleep while making love. Plus, you'll get kidnapped once a month or so. You might want to break up with me."

Donelle pursed her lips. "I'll have to think about it. A big public breakup might work, but you have to dump me. For now, let's see how it goes." She gave him a sly grin. "Wait, is rescue sex better than makeup sex?"

"Don't know, I've never been rescued. Should we try it on next month's kidnapping? If I figure out how to rescue anyone."

Laughing, Donelle picked up his hand and kissed it. "You rescued that woman from the diaper-bag snatching. Isn't that funny? In the middle of the night, at a police station, I realized how I felt. There I was…"

Sam put a finger on her lips. "I love you too." She had embraced the dreams and his narcolepsy, how could he not?

An uncomfortable silence fell. How did one follow that pronouncement? He leaned across the table and kissed her.

"Um, excuse me," the waitress said, standing beside their table, plates of hot food in her hands.

Embarrassed, Sam leaned back, making room. He didn't look at the waitress or Donelle. The knot of worry for her, his love, refused to leave his gut. If someone like the Purple Bouncer could find him, they could find Donelle too.

10
Silent Partner

A day or two later, Sam drifted off to sleep at work. The sleep lab materialized around him, except the room had a big window where twenty or thirty people watched him. How odd that he could get into a dream so fast.

"The advent of REM sleep occurs almost instantaneously. A variation so far from the norm, requires further study," Sam's mother said. She'd never used words like that in her life.

"Hey! I'm awake!" Sam said, a strange thought inside a dream. How can you sleep in a dream? What did this have to do with being a superhero anyway?

"The expectation of dreaming affects the ability to reach an enhanced dream state," his old pastor said, the father of the girl he'd gotten pregnant. "This is somewhat surprising, given his lack of faith in other areas of life."

"I have more faith than you! You old hypocrite!" They'd shipped her away to prevent him seeing her again, which made him furious.

"However," Sam's grandfather said. "His lack of ordinary sleep proves his lack of discipline. In the end, he wants to sleep at work, or he would sleep at night. Wake up! Sam, wake up!"

"Wha...huh?" Sam sat up in his office, blinking and confused.

Office Johns leaned over, with an odd smile on his face. "Hello, Sam, I'm afraid we need Narcolepsy."

Blinking at his police officer friend, Sam scowled. "You know my identity too?"

The smile did not leave his face. "We have resources, so it wasn't hard. Come on."

Sighing over more unfinished work, Sam locked his screen, grabbed his bag, and followed Officer Johns, who adopted a menacing scowl that said, "Don't get in my way," to anyone who might question his leaving with Sam. Together, they went out the back way toward the parking lot.

"What's going on?" Sam asked, breathless. "Don't you work nights?"

The squad car waited in the loading zone, lights flashing. "Yeah. It's an all-hands emergency. Where's your stuff?" Johns yawned as he hopped in.

Sam pointed to the lot across the way. "In my car."

Sensing the urgency, Sam jumped into the cruiser shotgun, and Johns drove him to his car, tires squealing. Then, while Johns raced through the streets, sirens and lights on, Sam tried to squeeze into his spandex. Johns headed for downtown but glanced over as Sam struggled with the stretchy fabric. "I should arrest you for indecent exposure."

"You could, but I'd have to fall asleep. What's going on?"

"You saw that viral footage from New York and Chicago?" Johns' voice stayed calm and even.

A chill went through Sam. "The Purple Bouncer." He'd come, just like Sam suspected. How could Sam fight him? The man could smash cars! The Favored Persons boys would sure want him. Being a hero meant facing impossible odds. Being a hero sucked. What could he do, though? Maybe he could give Purple a beer.

As he struggled to get the costume over his head, her realized he needed a hiding place. "Don't take me where he is. Like with the guy walking through walls, take me where he's going."

Nodding, Office Johns got on the radio and asked. The dispatcher replied that Purple had been spotted on the 16th Street Mall heading toward Broadway, but he'd turned South on Court Place.

"What's there?"

After thinking, Johns said, "The U.S. Mint."

They turned north on I-25, flew past cars and exited onto Colfax eastbound. At least three helicopters circled downtown, watching, filming, or guiding people on the ground. At midafternoon, the streets would be busy.

Sam got his costume buckled and twisted around to almost straight, only binding a little. He donned his mask and glasses, swallowed his fear, and prepared to exit the vehicle. "Let me off where he can't see."

They passed a police barricade, keeping back a curious throng. A block from the mint, Johns pulled over. Sam leaped out and walked east. The coursed stone building had an antique feel to it, with arched windows and decorative cornices, all surrounded by a low stone wall topped with a wrought-iron fence. Why would Purple attack here, since the place made coins, not bills? You couldn't carry enough away. Maybe it symbolized the world of banking and how the rich exploited the poor, or maybe Purple didn't know the place just made coins.

Federal guards had taken up places on the steps, with snipers on the roof. Tourists ran out the door. An RTD bus half flew, half slid from Court onto Colfax. It hit the curb and toppled. Sam scowled as he ran up to the door and into the mint's foyer.

A guard tried to stop him at the door to the offices. "Costumed clowns aren't allowed here."

Sam cocked his head. "I'll stop him, if I can."

The guard looked around as two more guys in suits came out the door. He shrugged. "What the hell? It's backwards day, isn't it? Welcome to the Denver Mint." He held the door for Sam.

Jogging down the corridor, Sam looked out the windows to see what the Purple Bouncer would do. He found one woman at her computer furiously typing. "Ma'am, you should leave."

"Why? Because some super-jerk is going to bust down the wall. The hell I will!"

Outside, the Purple Bouncer emerged from Court Street, bounced, picking up a parked car on his upward rebound. His momentum carried the car through the wrought iron fence and into the Mint's wall. Glass and stone rained down on the woman's desk, along with a broken taillight.

The woman growled. "Damn it! I need coffee." She rose and strode from the room like Patton going to war.

Sam sighed and crawled under her desk. He'd signed up to be a hero, so he needed to play out the scene. Changing his mind, Sam went back out in the hall. There, he peered around the corner into the office, watching and waiting. Despite the new hole in the wall, the Purple Bouncer would probably come in a different way. You could never predict supervillains, or superheroes. Sam sat against the wall in the corridor.

Sure enough, Purple bounced up to the roof among the snipers, who hadn't slowed him down anyway. Shouts and thuds followed, but no one fell off. One had to look for positives in these situations.

A huge crash shook the building, followed by a long silence, long enough for Sam to say, "What the hell?"

The roof caved in.

Sam rolled into a doorway. Amid the wood, stone, and roofing, Purple dropped to the floor. He crushed some debris but did not bounce. From his vantage in a little debris-lean-to, Sam could see one purple foot. The big guy didn't wear shoes. Sam couldn't resist. He reached out and tickled Purple's toes. "Coochie-coo!"

Purple jumped and bounced once before bending to grab Sam's hand. Sam, meanwhile, fought sleep—he dozed off fastest when trying to stay awake. His eyes drooped as Purple tried to pull him free.

The Denver mint faded away. A metallic clanking grew from a faint, far away echo to a loud hammering. A reddish, fiery glow illuminated dirty steel surroundings, girders, columns and roof covered with soot. Molten metal poured from a huge oven down into rectangular troughs. As it cooled, hammers beat it into shape, although some blows bounced as if the molten stuff might be rubber.

A regular-looking, not-purple guy stood beside Sam. "Where am I?"

Sam smirked. "Nothing to worry about. It's just a dream." The resemblance between the molten rubber and a volcano's lava gave Sam an idea. He reached into the flow and let the heat move up his arm. It turned him into a phoenix. As it did, the rubber river became a real river, with trees on the banks. The grass smoked beneath Sam's feet.

"What are you? A rubber chicken?"

Sam looked. Sure enough, he had magnificent, graceful, flaming, rubber wings. He'd walked into that one. "No, I'm a rubber Phoenix." He jumped, flapped his wings, and came down on not-Purple, except he stepped aside. Sam bounced. "Be nice, or I'll let my mom loose on you, or the Wicked Witch of the West. They might be the same."

Bouncing up into a tree, onto a boulder, and once off the stream itself, raising steam, Sam knocked not-Purple down. "Hey, this is fun."

"Why are you doing this to me?" Not-Purple asked. "I'm a good guy! I only harass the rich, and I give away lots of money."

Sam landed, but before he could answer, a loud bang interrupted him. Pain lanced through his side. Was that a gunshot? The dream faded.

~~~~

Jenna found a laundry cart in a hotel on the north end of Colorado Springs after checking in. She dragged Noah from the car and into the basket and added the heavy money bags before covering both with towels. In Colorado's thin air, she had to stop and catch her breath. Still breathing hard, she heaved the basket. The automatic door opened for her, letting her push him inside. No one gave her a second glance as she took the freight elevator to her room, unloaded, and returned the cart.

With Noah unconscious, she'd decided not to go far. After sitting on the other bed for a while, she reached over and slapped him. "Why won't you wake up? Who was that guy, anyway?"

The rush from shooting the hero guy in gray spandex faded slowly. She didn't think she'd killed him, although he might have bled out. Some guards had come up, and she'd had to get Noah away. Earlier, with all the attention on Noah, she'd managed to grab four bags of dollar coins and raid their little display of its most valuable pieces. On her way out of town, she'd dumped one bag's contents at a park shelter where a bunch of kids had been playing baseball.

She slapped Noah again. That felt good, to have so much power over him. She could leave him, but a distraction helped keep people from noticing her. On her own, Jenna did well enough, but Noah could break open vaults before he let someone chase him away.

Jenna rose and paced the little room. What to do? What to do? Now she wished she'd taken more time and smashed that moron's face in, rather than just shoot him, but then she would have had to leave Noah. If she hadn't put him in the cart, Noah would have been noticeable. Damn, damn, damn.

First, she would count their money. If Jenna had to leave him, she would take it all, but would it be enough to retire on, unnoticed? On the other hand, the guy in gray seriously messed with their day. A plan for revenge grew in Jenna's mind.

11
Waking

Dr. Giles ran to the elevator and jabbed the down button. She had to get to surgery. "Come on, come on, come on." After waiting two seconds, she turned and dashed for the stairs.

She'd arrived for her normal evening shift of insomniacs and people with serial nightmares, and the rumor mill reported Sam had come back into the emergency room. Ignoring HIPAA rules, Dr. Giles checked out his chart. He'd been shot, and they had him scheduled for emergency surgery. Swearing, Dr. Giles headed down from the sleep lab to the OR suite.

When she reached the ground floor, she pushed an intern aside and crashed through the double-doors into the surgical ward. Spinning left, she skimmed past a scrub nurse with a sterile tray. Another nurse yelled at her while Dr. Giles scanned the board. She bounced off a surgeon, knocking his sandwich into the air. Dr. Giles caught the ham and swiss on rye like a wide receiver and made a hand-off to an attending. They'd assigned Sam to Dr. Stanwick. Best damned trauma surgeon in the state, and the most arrogant. Warnings did not apply.

Bursting into the surgical suite, Dr. Giles slid to a stop on the threshold, outside the sterile field. "Stop!" Her next words died on her tongue as Dr. Stanwick laid a hand on the sterile sheet covering Sam to steady his scalpel. Instead of cutting, he slumped, planting his face in Sam's belly. The scrub nurse reached over to shake his shoulder and fell asleep before sliding to the floor. The anesthesiologist appeared to have some sense, or he'd read the chart. He left oxygen tubing there and sat back to watch his monitors.

Dr. Giles rolled her eyes and turned back to the corridor. All the patients, orderlies, nurses, providers, and even a janitor there stared at her. "Is there another trauma surgeon around? This one's broken."

The charge nurse checked to find a surgeon, so Dr. Giles retrieved the surgical robot. As she wheeled it past the desk, she said, "Find someone who can wield this thing."

People should read her warnings. She didn't put them there for her own amusement.

The next day, when Sam, not to mention the surgeon, scrub nurse, and four people from the ER, hadn't woken up, Dr. Giles went to Sam's room, Curiosity won over sound medical practice. She should wait for Donelle, but she wanted to find out herself. Since the first time she'd seen him, she'd been distracted, her thoughts often returning to Narcolepsy. His ability intrigued her on a professional level.

The room had a recliner, since many patients slept better in one, so Dr. Giles dragged it close to the bed. With a sigh, she leaned her head back, brought the foot support up, and took Sam's hand.

~~~~~

Later, how long Sam couldn't tell, he wandered through a stone-walled maze. How did he get here? Where had Not-Purple gotten to? The place smelled of antiseptic and alcohol. When he found the exit, bright light shining in, he hurried out, into another maze. The white, sterile walls looked familiar, but not the shape or the pattern. He needed to find Not-Purple. He needed to escape somehow. Donelle would be worried.

Sam kept wandering, looking for a way out. Once in a while he met other people, all medical professionals. None of them knew where to go or what to do either. Footsteps approached. "Purple? Is that you?" The echoing footfalls said not.

Dr. Giles turned a corner and smiled. "There you are. It's time to wake up, Sam."

"Wait, why are you here? Am I in the hospital again? Where's Donelle?"

Smiling, Dr. Giles shrugged. "We sent her home to get some sleep. You recovered enough for us to try this before she got back. Plus, I wanted to know how much control you have."

Sam blinked. "What? Recovered from what? Control over what?"

"Let's walk." She led him back through the maze. "Your dreams, of course. For instance, can you change our surroundings here?"

"I don't understand what you mean." Sam walked around a corner into the haunted forest, bare trees looming over them. Purple might be in a place like this, but there could be flying monkeys.

Flying monkeys screeched overhead.

Dr. Giles looked around, eyes wide. "Like that. Very...interesting."

A monkey swooped down at her, and Sam swatted it from the air, only realizing he'd turned to the rubber phoenix again when Dr. Giles stared at him rather than the surroundings. Sam took a deep breath and turned back into himself. "Sorry."

"A rubber chicken?"

"It's a rubber phoenix!"

Dr. Giles laughed. "Or course it is. I believe you've answered the first question, though. You have control, quite good control. Now we should wake up."

Sam looked around. "Can't. We have to find the not-so-Purple Bouncer first, not to mention those other people."

Dr. Giles looked puzzled. "The police didn't find anyone with you this time."

Sam paused. What had happened? "Oh, he's here, and I have to be touching him when I wake up. Wherever he is, he's asleep, and he won't wake if I don't find him here. That is, I think he won't. It's always been touch to get into the dream, and touch to get out." What would happen if he didn't touch someone here to wake them up?

If Dr. Giles had come in, and Donelle had needed sleep, Sam had been unconscious for days. Had she waited for Donelle to leave? Sam doubted Donelle would have agreed to let Dr. Giles come into Sam's dreams. The good doctor had not asked or even mentioned her intention. Why did she need to know if he controlled his dreams?

Dr. Giles laughed. "Well, then, go where he is."

Sam blinked a moment, thoughts having drifted far from Purple. Without thinking, Sam turned left and headed uphill. After winding through some rocks and plastic trees, they came to a creepy castle. Monkeys with strangely stiff joints flew around the towers above. The walls and fanged portcullis had a plastic sheen to them, but why didn't penetrate until they got to the bridge over the mote. Dr. Giles stopped, looking at the round knobs atop the gray bridge railing. "A Lego castle?"

Blinking, Sam looked again at the monkeys—flying Lego monkeys, and Lego guards prowling the walls. "Well, sometimes you have to use the materials at hand." Halfway across the bridge, Sam stopped and shuddered. He'd seen this castle before. He'd built it as a kid, and it had given him nightmares at age six. Setting his jaw, he walked through the ominous plastic gate into the toy darkness beyond. The monkey's screeching echoed from above.

As soon as they cleared the gate, not-Purple ran up to them. "How did you get through the gate?" When a monkey dove toward the courtyard, he took a swipe at it, knocking it aside. "I hate those things, I want to smash them. Why can't I smash things here?"

Not-Purple headed for the gate, but the portcullis slammed down with a light click, plastic grating on polished plastic. "Damn it, I want out! I'm a good guy!"

Sam shook his head. "First, you are a thief, not a good guy. If want to oppose the rich, find a different way. Second, you need to stop being so mean. Third, it's my dream. Fourth, they're Legos." He grabbed the portcullis and pulled. It bent, then the seams widened until the pieces separated and the whole gate tinkled to the ground.

When they stepped outside, the guards shot plastic arrows at them, which bounced, though they did sting a little. The flying monkeys dove on them. Purple ripped a section of bridge rail off and took a swing at the closest. Sam turned back into the rubber phoenix-chicken and swatted them from the air. The last one flying, however, sprouted a real head—Sergeant Willis's head.

When Purple tried hit him, Sam grabbed the Lego club. "Not him."

Willis flapped down to land on the bridge railing. "Legos and a rubber phoenix? Man, your dreams are strange places."

Sam gave in to the silliness. "It's a rubber...never mind."

Willis scratched his nose with a plastic paw. "Wait a minute, I'm off duty..."

Sam blinked. He not only didn't have a bad guy for Willis to arrest outside the dream, Willis hadn't been near the hospital. Every time he dreamed, he knew less. How much did he control?

"Are there any others?" Willis said.

Sam landed, turning back into himself. He gestured toward the good doctor. "Dr. Giles says there are some others. I did end up in the hospital." To not-Purple he pointed a thumb. "This is the bad guy, the Purple Bouncing one, but we only have him here, not in the real world."

Sergeant Willis hopped down from the bridge and up to not-Purple. "This is the guy terrorizing all the banks throughout the country? He doesn't look like much here."

Not-Purple looked like he might take Willis apart, and since Willis had a Lego body, he might be able to. Sam held not-Purple back and took his club away. "I said, stop being so mean!"

The remaining, confused monkeys circled overhead. As soon as Sam reached dry rock, he stopped. "Who are these other people? I met a few medical types."

Dr. Giles counted on her fingers. "Two EMTs, an ER resident, an ER nurse, a scrub nurse, and a surgeon."

Scowling, Sam looked around. Where would they be? Why had he seen them so seldom? Outside or in the castle they would be easy to find. "They must be in the maze, which seemed like a hospital." He strode across the barren wastelands until the maze formed around them, along with the astringent odor. White walls and floors turned blind corners into dead-ends or wound through impossible gyrations. After three or four false starts, Sam put hands on hips. This is ridiculous." Turning back into the rubber chicken, Sam lifted off the ground. "Phoenix smash!"

He rammed into the wall and bounced.

Not-Purple guffawed. "No, idiot. You're rubber. You bounce. It'll come down."

Sam glared. He didn't like bad guys pointing out his idiocy. Folding his wings, he dropped to the floor and bounced. His angle sent him into the far wall, and he adjusted a little to go back and forth between the two. It was his dream, damn it, no walls could stop him.

He picked up speed while Willis and Giles ducked. Both walls shattered. White plastic caromed from floor and ceiling. Sam dropped and spread his wings over his friends. The walls fell like dominos. They sprouted spots and a line down the middle—the one-two, the six-three, more and more. At the far end, the tiles split around people in scrubs.

Sergeant Willis followed the tiles around as Sam led not-Purple and Dr. Giles over to the others.

A man in scrubs harangued the others and pointed at a woman. "Do it again. You're next. We will get out of this place."

The woman he pointed at spread her arms to the fallen dominos. "Um, the maze is gone. We can walk out."

"My plan is working! Come on."

Sam shook his head as walked up. "Who is that guy?"

Grimacing, Dr. Giles sighed. "A brilliant trauma surgeon. Would have saved your life if he'd read your chart and seen my note."

"You mean I'm dead?" Sam asked.

Sergeant Willis laughed while Dr. Giles shook her head. "The second doctor listened and used the surgical robot. Touching though cloth makes you sleep, but the robot is operated like a computer game, from a joystick console."

There she went analyzing his sleep again. Creepy. To avoid thinking about Giles, Sam walked over to the surgeon. "I knocked down the dominos, and I can even make it rain."

Thunder clapped overhead. A downpour drenched them all.

Sam turned his face up and let the water run over his face. "Gather around! It's time to go home!"

The surgeon, ignoring the rain on his face, folded his arms. "My work knocked down the dominos."

Sam paid no attention and tried to take Not-Purple's hand, but he pulled away. "What are you doing? I'm not helping you."

Shrugging, Sam turned away. "Fine with me. Just stay here. Everyone, gather around."

Not-Purple grabbed Sam's hand and tried to crush it. "I tell you, I'm a good guy. Next time I see you, I'm to going smash you into a pancake."

"Ooh, I like pancakes. Are you going to bring syrup?"

Dr. Giles took his other hand and the scrub nurse's too. Everyone joined in except the surgeon.

"You can stay here if you want." Sam took a deep breath and wondered how to wake up this time. "Ollie ollie outs-in-free! Wake up, wake up, wherever you are!" As the dominoes faded and the dream-ground shook, the surgeon jumped in and pulled everyone down into a pile.

~~~~

Groaning, Sam blinked. A regular hospital room came into focus, much plainer than the sleep lab room. Dr. Giles snatched her hand from his, as if embarrassed. Even so, she schooled her features and took his vitals. Pain throbbed up Sam's side. He put his hand there and found a plastic water-proof bandage. Tubes from an IV hindered his movements. "What?"

Dr. Giles shone a light in his eyes. "Pain meds coming up. The police found you in a bloody pool with no one else around. Someone shot you twice at close range. From what you said, you must have been asleep at the time."

"And the shooter dragged Purple away." Sam grimaced. Breathing hurt. He tried to stay calm, to ease the pain in his side. "How...how did everyone miss the fact that Purple had a partner?"

"Don't ask me. Denver police, the FBI, and those feds from before all want to talk—"

Another doctor walked in. "And I am the gatekeeper. They talk to you when and how long I say."

Dr. Giles stepped back, deferring to this guy, which made Sam distrust him. "This is the doctor who reads warnings."

He repeated Dr. Giles' light-in-the-eye thing, then probed a bit at the wound and surrounding area. He picked up a bag Sam hadn't noticed, examining the murky liquid inside. "Hmm. I'm glad you're awake. That's a good sign. See you tomorrow." He swept out, stopped, and turned back to Sam from the doorway. "If anyone you don't want tries to get in, tell the nurse and she'll contact me."

Dr. Giles stood against the wall, arms folded as the surgeon departed. "He may be an ass, but he can use a surgical robot. I would suggest waiting until tomorrow to talk to the police."

Sam considered. "If Officer Johns is out there, send him in. No one else, except Donelle."

"Of course. That button there gives you pain meds and regulates the amount." Dr. Giles smiled. "Thank you for sharing your dream with me. I learned a great deal."

As Sam reached for the pain button, Dr. Giles departed. It didn't take long for a shouting match to break out in the corridor. Sam imagined Dr. Giles holding back the feds and giggled. Officer Johns slipped in and shut the door behind.

"How are you doing?" Johns looked worried.

Sam giggled again. "I got morphine. Feel better." It took effect fast through an IV.

Johns laughed. "Are you lucid enough to tell me what happened? All we know is we found you shot with no sign of the Purple Bouncer."

Sam struggled to put words together and waved his arm trying to make a point. "Purple came with me. I got him. Someone else shot me."

Johns scowled. "I'll talk to the detectives, but no one saw anyone, and there must have been fifty or sixty cops there."

"Yesss...someone else. Sleep now."

Johns patted his arm. "Get better." He walked out muttering to himself. "All he does is sleep."

Except when he wanted to, then Sam couldn't sleep. He lay in the hospital bed, mind whirling and trying to remember a partner, even though he couldn't put a coherent thought together.

~~~~

Jenna sat in the soft chair in the hotel room, laptop on her knees as she traced who Narcolepsy might be. He'd made the news a few times and rode with the cops. He'd captured several supervillains, and he'd gotten in a bar fight with two powered people. All three had ended up in the hospital. She found that odd Westword site, and the article about the Favored Persons Act. The law sent a chill down her spine. The government could make her vanish.

Blinking, Jenna chuckled. She could make herself vanish. No way the government could hold her.

Noah screamed and sat up in bed. He screamed again, leaped from the bed and turned purple. With a jump, he hit the roof, bouncing back and forth between floor and ceiling. Plaster rained down. Concrete cracked. Jenna made herself small, unseen and unnoticed. She wished she could open a window, but she cranked up the AC in anticipation.

After his third bounce, Noah calmed down. He shouted again, this time in frustration, and exhaled. The stink billowed through the room. "What the fuck did he do to me?" Noah sat on the bed, putting head in hands. "What did he do? I'll smash him, I will."

Jenna concluded Noah had no sense of smell. "What happened?" she asked.

Noah looked up but couldn't find her. He rolled his eyes and stared into the distance. "When I collapsed the roof, he hid under the rubble and tickled me. I pulled him out, and I don't know. We both landed in this weird steel mill, well rubber mill. He touched the molten rubber and turned into this winged, fiery rubber chicken. I ran, and I got away, but the flying monkeys came for me and took me to a Lego castle. They screamed all night long. I couldn't sleep and I couldn't get out. It lasted forever. In the end, he came back, with this woman, and...well, he knocked down the domino maze, we held hands, and I woke up here."

The fear in Jenna's belly at his uncontrolled anger loosened. She let him see her, though she might need a new partner if Noah couldn't control his temper. "I found you asleep with that guy, so I shot him and lugged you into the cart. Man, that thing was heavy, with you and the coins. Then I walked out and came here. You held hands?" The news said Narcolepsy had been hurt, but not how badly. She had managed to convert the coins to higher denominations and deposit them. "I suspect you woke when he did, though miles away. How strange."

"If I see that damned Narcolepsy, I'll squash him."

Jenna took a deep breath. Sometimes she imagined a man who would protect her, but no such man existed. "We have to choose between stealing more money for our retirement where no one can bother us or getting revenge on Narcolepsy."

"Revenge," Noah said.

12
Recovery

Donelle stood, hands on hips, glaring at Sam, who sat on the hospital bed. "Dr. Giles joined your dream and got you to wake up?"

Sam wanted to go home. Perhaps he should have waited to tell Donelle. "She said she wanted to find out if I could control the dreams."

Rolling her eyes, Donelle knelt to help get him dressed. "Of course, you can control the dreams. Think about the silent beach."

Remembering the beach, that he, who had never been to the sea, dreamed, Sam laughed, then doubled over in pain. "Ow. Don't make me laugh. Ow." He ended lying on the bed again.

The nurse with the wheelchair and release paperwork showed up. "Are we ready to go home?"

"Yes," Sam said. He and Donelle struggled to get his pants and shoes on while the nurse watched, grinning the whole time.

"Nice legs," the nurse said.

It hurt getting in the wheelchair, but not badly. Sam didn't feel well enough to go home, but he couldn't wait to get away from the hospital bed—the poor food, the noise, the smells, the needles. Every time he tried to sleep, a nurse or doctor came in to poke or prod or ask questions. How are you feeling? Can't sleep? Take two of these. How's your blood pressure doing? That bag is about empty. I'll get you a new one. Need the bedpan? Just making rounds, don't worry about me. Need another blanket? Here, let me turn out the light. When he ran out of water, then they didn't come.

The drive home proved to be moving from one pain to another, even though Donelle drove like a little old grandma.

Not Sam's grandma. She drove like Dale Earnhardt. When they got to the apartment, the walk from parking lot to elevator looked like a climb up Mt. Everest. Donelle helped, though, and they went slow. When they reached the door, Sam heard it unlock. The click relaxed him.

"You're home," Donelle said. "Bed or couch?"

Sam wanted to sit on the couch and veg out with the TV. His body had other ideas. "Bed."

When he lay down on his own bed, Sam ran a hand over his sheets. "Ah, that's what they meant. We heal better at home." Sam's heart sank. "I'm supposed to be a superhero. We aren't supposed to get laid up. I'm not supposed to be so vulnerable."

Donelle laid down beside him. "True, but you're new at this. What did you learn?"

Sam considered. "That Purple has a partner, and I can't go to sleep until I account for everyone."

Snuggling up against him, Donelle nodded. "What happens if you get famous, if the villains all know what you do? Purple does."

Donelle's perfume and her warmth against his arm distracted Sam, so he took a couple breaths. "It means he'll try to pound me as soon as he sees me." As he tried to concentrate, his eyes fluttered.

"Don't you fall asleep on me, now," Donelle said, with laughter in her voice.

Sam struggled to stay awake, but soon he found himself standing in a windswept pasture astride a horse or a dragon. Either way, he rode bareback and naked.

"What's with all the animals?" Donelle said.

He looked over. She rode beside him on a white Pegasus, also naked. "What? You have something against winged horses?" As he spoke, both mounts flapped and jumped off the ground. "Let's go mess around on a cloud."

The ground fell away and they flitted through the sky. Sam picked a fluffy white mound and guided his horse over. Donelle circled as he dismounted, only landing after Sam didn't fall through. Grinning, she leapt from her mount, landing in the swirling mist. She took two tentative steps, jumped, and wrapped her legs around his waist.

~~~~

The next day, Sam binged on Purple Bouncer videos. The guy had gotten famous. Witnesses to his escapades had posted video from robberies in New York, Chicago, and St. Louis, even a couple from rich kids as their houses got smashed. In each case, he broke in somewhere but left with no loot, or if he did, like in New York, he dropped it out in the open.

A partner's presence couldn't have been clearer. Either that, or Purple took the prize as the stupidest thief ever; he never stole anything. Sam watched the videos again and again, looking for someone else.

Finding his burner phone beside his Internet-radio-alarm-clock, he started dialing Officer Johns but changed his mind. He fished in the drawer in his nightstand and found the card for the Favored Persons Fed. Who else would have access to the street cameras from at least three different cities? Thinking it through, Sam set up a one-time soft-phone on his laptop. Even as he dialed, he knew he would regret it. "Hello, Agent Jones. This is Narcolepsy."

"Who?"

"Uh, Narcolepsy. We met at the hospital when you took Laser Guy and Yellow Blur."

"Oh! He didn't tell you? This is a clearing house. We're all agent Jones here. Hold on." This new Jones typed a bit. "Ah. You're the one we classified as useless, just a recruiter."

Sam rolled his eyes, wishing this Jones could see it. Maybe they had some other Jones spying on him. "Useless? I've already caught four guys for you, and I'm just getting started."

"We can catch them ourselves, especially as we…so why did you call the hotline? I see you got shot going up against the purple guy."

Did they need to know this? They already did. "Yes. I took down Purple, then got shot."

Agent Jones didn't answer right away. "I'm confused. You got him, but he shot you?"

"No, I got him, and his partner shot me. A partner no one even knows is there, and who no one saw. Watch all the videos, I think you'll see. I hoped you could get me street cams and the like for all Purple's robberies."

Again, Unknown Agent Jones hesitated. "A partner no one can see. So, what happened to Purple?" The Feds hadn't figured that out. Someone hadn't put obvious clues together. Then again, Sam had only seen it when he looked at all the robberies. Each city might have missed it.

"His partner took him away. I expect he woke when I did."

"I'll get you whatever footage I can scrounge, and we'll look for ourselves. Just one favor, though. When Purple strikes again, we want you to take him on. We'll even provide transport if needed."

There it was, favor for favor, and him beginning to work with the Feds. More, Purple would squash him next time, meaning Sam had to avoid the bouncer and capture a partner who couldn't be seen. No problem. "Well, I doubt I'll be able to fool Purple next time, but if you can get me there in time, I'm in." He needed someone to watch his back.

~~~~

A week later, Sam felt much better. He hobbled into the martial arts studio with Donelle, both already wearing their gi. Master Ray Elegion came over, and Sam gave a stiff bow.

Ray raised an eyebrow. "What happened to you?"

"I got shot. Turns out taking one bad guy into my dream while a second is around is a bad idea."

Ray laughed. "Good observation." He bowed to Donelle. "Hello. What might I do for you?"

Donelle looked taken aback. She blinked then shrugged. "If I'm going to hang out with this guy, I need to be able to defend myself."

"Against people bigger, faster, and stronger," Ray said, stepping out onto the mat.

"Much." Donelle slipped off her shoes and followed, circling Ray like a cat on the prowl.

Rather than join them, Sam closed his eyes. "I need to fight someone I can't see, or don't notice. And get back in fighting shape, in fact, better fighting shape."

"Ok," Ray said, moving across the room on quiet feet. "We start with the regular moves in slow motion, so you don't hurt yourself." He opened a drawer across the way, near the wall, rummaged in it, and walked back.

When he drew close, Sam could feel his presence, perhaps a warmth against his skin. When Ray reached out, Sam executed a block, surprised when he connected with Ray's arm—so surprised, he opened his eyes.

Ray stood with a black cloth held like he wanted to wrap it around Sam's head, looking amused, annoyed, and surprised all at once. Mastering himself, Ray stepped forward again. "Eyes open involuntarily. If you want to learn this, you need a blindfold."

The hour-long session had Sam going through the same motions as always, except slower and blind. He listened, heard soft footsteps, felt shifts in the air. His wound snagged a time or two, but his surgeon had said movement induced the body to heal—as if motion told his body to hurry up already.

Sam did the entire hour in a blindfold, listening to Ray's light step and Donelle's breathing, gauging distance and considering what he might do. Four times, Ray came close. Three times, Sam missed it altogether or heard too late, erasing the euphoria from the first success. The last time, when Ray came near, Sam ducked away. Not great, but good enough.

When they walked out, Donelle took his arm. Sam thought he could walk better than on the way in. His side hurt, but with a stretchy pain. Even so, his muscles felt tired and a little sore. "It's going to take a while to get back to form."

Donelle cocked her head as she walked around to the driver's side of her Forester. "What will you do if someone attacks before then?"

With hand on the cool door, Sam paused. Why would the bad guys wait for him to get better? They wouldn't. "Talk them out of it."

Donelle snorted.

When he came, Purple wouldn't wait to listen.

13
The Weigh-in

Days later, Donelle made her weary way up to her apartment, considering popcorn and Pepsi for supper. She'd made it through another day catering to attorneys. Today had included an, "I'm thinking of a document, a letter from someone in Pennsylvania," task. Donelle had found that damned document.

She got out her keys as she approached the second-floor, missing Sam's automatic unlocking door. The hall smelled of new carpet. It looked like the landlords finally gotten around to that. The workmen had scratched her door and the lock, or had it been someone else? The hairs on her neck stood up. The damage might not mean anything. Even so, she unlocked the door and pushed it open without moving inside. Down the hall in her living room, someone rose from the couch.

Donelle ran.

Two steps down the hall, she collided with someone she hadn't noticed, a confused impression of fabric and skin. When she landed on her back, the big purple guy emerged from her apartment and loomed over her. She tried to scoot away down the hall.

Purple jumped, bouncing off ceiling and floor. Plaster rained down.

Donelle went aggressive and kicked up to her feet. Before meeting Sam, she couldn't have done that. Even so, she backed away, keeping her knees bent, her arms up and ready. She tried not to let her doubt and fear show. He looked like a big rubber ball, and Donelle had played volleyball in school.

Laughing, Purple bounced toward her. Donelle braced her arms and bumped him toward the setter, more a deflection than anything. The force pushed her down, almost squatting. Purple changed direction, even though her arms felt like they'd hit a concrete wall.

Purple stopped laughing. He bounced to the end of the hall.

"One-nothing," Donelle said, shaking out her arms.

On his way back, Purple wreaked havoc on the apartment building. With the plaster gone in places, concrete dust rained down. He adjusted his trajectory too. He'd be coming up when he got to her.

Donelle squatted and used a two-hand set, half volleyball, half Krav Maga. Purple's momentum pushed her down on her ass, but he flew up and over. "Side out. Two-nothing." The Krav Maga moves worked, even if Ray called her sloppy.

As she prepared for the next serve, Donelle wanted to rub her butt, but it would give away he'd hurt her. A misdirection could help, though. Moving to the center of the hall, Donelle dragged her right leg.

After two failed attempts to squash her, Purple stopped near the stairs and considered his next move. He spoke, keeping his voice low. Who was he talking to? Purple jumped at an angle, bouncing in a square as he approached.

Donelle, in a volleyball bump stance, took a step back and watched him come. This would be awkward, both angle and timing. She took a step forward and dived along the wall. The carpet stopped her slide and she glimpsed her own leg sticking out across the floor. "Sloppy." Purple came down on her calf, shattering the bone with a loud crack.

Purple put his feet down and stopped. Before he could speak, Donelle shouted, "Timeout!" She didn't want to admit a two-to-one score.

A voice from nowhere said, "If you're done playing games, take her inside."

Purple picked up Donelle. Her leg flopped in ways a leg shouldn't flop. Pain hit her like a freight train in the rain on a plain. Consciousness faded away, even as she wished for one of Sam's dreams.

~~~~

Sam sat on his couch, streaming a dark fantasy that's best bit was boobs. He didn't pay much attention. He had his laptop out too, scrolling through Facebook and random web pages. He hurt, and he missed Donelle. He hated it when she worked late and couldn't see him. Getting up, he went to the fridge and stood with the door open, looking for food, finding only unappetizing remnants.

Over the last week or more, Sam had put himself through boot camp when not at work—exercising twice a day, thrice on weekends, to make up for lost time. His wound hurt, though, and he had to adjust his movements to accommodate. He missed going out with Officer Johns, but he didn't feel ready yet.

His phone chimed with a text. His heart raced when he saw Donelle's message. "Hi. Can you cum over? I'm kinda down."

Even as he rose to find pants, Sam frowned. The wording didn't sound like Donelle, but after showering, he dressed, shut down his electronics, and went regardless. Outside, the night had turned cool, but no longer cold. It felt good on his hot skin. He stood breathing in the crisp air, sharp in his lungs.

A police cruiser screamed around the corner and slid to a stop, two wheels up on the curb. The passenger window went down and Officer Johns leaned over. "Get in, Kid. We found Purple."

Sam thumbed toward the parking lot. "My stuff's in my car." He jogged to the lot, grabbed his gym bag from the back seat, and hopped in the cruiser, which Johns had helpfully backed up right next the parking lot.

Before Sam even had the door closed, Johns gunned it in reverse. He cranked the wheel, spun the car around, slamming the door shut, and took off forward without stopping. With the cruiser whipping around almost-stopped cars, Sam disrobed and pulled on his spandex. "Why do these costumes have to be spandex? Who thought of this?"

Officer Johns chuckled, but it had a serious edge to it. "It's funnier still watching you put it on. We have a situation, though." He did not sound amused as he touched the screen on his car computer. "Purple is here." An address popped up.

Sam stared, pants half way up his legs and one arm squeezing through a tight sleeve. "That's…oh, fuck. Donelle's apartment. She just texted me to come over." Fear and fury went to war in Sam's gut and chest. He wanted to hurt someone, a foreign feeling, and he wanted to run and hide.

Shaking his head, Johns whistled. "Smells like a trap set for you. I get the impression he doesn't like you."

"Not just him, them. He has a partner." Sam mulled over Donelle's two-bedroom apartment, with Purple, who would not fall for Sam's tricks again, and whoever shot him lying in wait. "I'm going to need help."

Officer Johns didn't answer as he barreled east on Sixth Avenue. He slowed to negotiate an intersection, swerving into the oncoming lanes to get around cars stopped at the light. "I don't know what we can do for you. We can't stop Purple. Are you sure he has a partner?"

"Look at the videos. He's never once gotten away with any loot."

Johns gaped, then snapped his gaze back to the road as he swerved to avoid a delivery truck, followed by another swerve for the required woman with a baby stroller in the crosswalk.

Sam came to a reluctant conclusion. "I have to ask the feds."

Office Johns grumbled. "I don't like them taking all the people with powers."

Sam punched the buttons on his pre-paid. Today's agent Jones, a woman, answered. "National Security Desk, Agent Jones speaking. How may I help you?"

Sam launched his plea. "Hi, Agent Jones, this is Narcolepsy. Change of plan. I take you to the Purple Bouncer. He and his partner are here, with a hostage. I need help."

Jones chuckled, but with little mirth. "Wait, will you owe us a favor for helping or would we owe you for helping us get Purple? Text me the address. I'll see what I can do. What do you need?"

"Um, what aspect of national security does this desk cover?"

"The secure aspects."

Sam fumed at the meaningless non-answer. "Um…do you take security tips?"

Agent Jones, not Jessica, brightened. "Of course! First, who is calling?"

Why would they need to know that for a tip? "I'm Narcolepsy. I'll give you a moment to look it up." Sam hummed the Jeopardy theme.

Ms. Jones typed in fits and starts. "Stop that. How do I know you're Narcolepsy anyway?"

Johns laughed, and Sam did too. "I'm the lamest superhero in town. Who would claim to be me?"

"Sir," Jones said, not amused. "Without identity verification, threat assessment and target value cannot be determined."

"Now you're reading from a script. Are you a new agent? Did they stick you with the most boring duty?"

"I will have you know I am a fully qualified agent, trained for these situations. All the responses, all the duties, every eventuality."

"Ms. Jones, if you are dealing with superheroes and villains, nothing will be as you expect. Nothing. For instance, today, the Purple Bouncer is here in Denver. He and his partner have taken a hostage. Check with dispatch and send everyone you can to assist catching Purple. I..." He wanted to say he couldn't do it alone but thought better of it. "…thought you might want Purple in your secret army. Maybe I was wrong, though. His partner has an ability too, to walk unnoticed. That could be the perfect spy for you, but if you aren't interested, don't send anyone. I'm sure the local police can handle it, though no one has been able to catch him yet."

"Sir, our unit is not ready for…"

Sam had to resist chuckling. Not ready for what? Publicity? Field operations? "Don't worry about Purple's peculiar partner, who wouldn't be any use to you anyway."

"Sir, if you will hang on…"

Sam hung up on her.

Officer Johns laughed. "My sergeant won't be happy about letting the feds in." Johns turned south for a few blocks before heading East on Alameda.

Sam knew Johns was right. Upsetting the local police did not seem wise but rescuing Donelle took precedence. "Unless Phase-boy is still in custody, or you know some other costumed clown, we need help only these Agent Jones's can offer."

Johns shook his head. "That Phase Boy kid vanished before the feds showed up to take him away."

The comment struck a chord with Sam—not the escaping, but the kid part. He didn't know why people had these powers now, but Yellow and Laser-guy had been Sam's age. Tickler had been younger, as had Phase-boy. He couldn't guess an age for Purple, but were they all under thirty? What had happened to them as kids? Probably pesticides.

They pulled up at Donelle's building where twelve other patrol cars, two swat armored personnel carriers, and a command truck had the place surrounded. Two police choppers and at least one news helicopter circled overhead, not to mention a dozen drones. A robot moved back and forth on the sidewalk—probably remote control, not autonomous. Plastic barricades cordoned the spectators, who pushed close. A firetruck and two ambulances sat out on the road, waiting. The police had occupied themselves with clearing the building, hence the crowd.

When Sam emerged from the car, wearing his spandex and mask, the gnawing worry for Donelle overwhelmed him. He dashed into the building. He had to save Donelle. The crowd behind the barricades cheered. In the stairwell, plaster littered the treads and concrete dust settled over it all. Sam slid across the floor. Who would pay if Purple smashed through a wall or brought the building down?

The incongruous thought stopped Sam before he put a foot on the first step. Running in without a plan could be fatal., or at least hurt a lot. More, he needed to wait for the feds. His body wanted action, wanted to hit something, or someone, or at least a wall. Fighting to stand still, Sam forced himself to look back out the door.

Officer Johns went over to the sergeant who had given Sam a hard time that first night, out of sight from Donelle's apartment. Wait. Would Purple have seen Sam go in? A wicked grin grew on Sam's face. He slipped back out, staying close to the wall so Purple and Partner couldn't see him. Let them wait and stew on why he didn't dash upstairs to rescue Donelle.

Purple and Partner didn't want to take over the world. Who would want to take that on anyway? They wanted to be like Robin Hood, except they kept more than they gave away. Did they want the people on their side? Worry about people thinking they were bad guys?

When he considered what to do next, he noticed the command truck, parked well away from the windows. It had antennae on top and power cables running to outside plugs on the building. Intrigued, Sam walked over, climbed the three steps, knocked, and went in without waiting for an answer. He needed to keep his mind off Donelle. Plus, he wanted to see what tech the police had. If they got pissed, he could pretend he didn't know any better.

In the dark van, two men sat at computer screens built into the wall. The place smelled of coffee, electronics, and French fries. One man in a suit paced, one step each way, while wearing a headset. "Yes, we're trying to locate Narcolepsy for you. He should arrive soon." Glancing at Sam, he rolled his eyes and turned away. "We'll need something from you before we send him up. How about you let us send in a paramedic? You don't need a hostage now."

Pulling up a stool next to a uniformed officer who had what looked like an infrared view of the apartment, Sam identified Purple with ease. He looked more like a giant beachball than a person as he bounced around. Someone lay in Donelle's bed. A chill went through Sam. If they needed paramedics, she must be hurt. If he got these two into his dreams, no more mister nice guy.

The surveillance officer glanced at Sam and whispered, "Are you Narcolepsy?"

Sam nodded but kept his voice low. "Can your software identify how many people it thinks are in a room?"

"Sure." He typed a few keys, and a grid formed over the infrared image. Little cursors tracked heat and movement both. When the software chimed, it read, "3 subjects on premise." The officer nodded and pointed at the screen. "There you are, three. One here, and one there on the bed. No problem." The man hadn't even noticed the third person.

Impressive. Purple's partner had real power. Sam tried to work through scenarios on how get to Purple a second time. He didn't know why Purple wouldn't just flatten him. Sam's power had a serious flaw with repeat customers.

The negotiator pressed a button on the headset and tossed it on a chair. "Nothing doing on releasing the hostage. He wants you, Narcolepsy."

Sam stood. "I figured. We have history. What would you do if you were facing someone who knew all your tricks?"

He laughed. "Develop new tricks." He paused. "No, that isn't true. I would use his knowledge against him. If he knew my techniques, I could anticipate his reactions."

That made sense. Purple wouldn't want Sam to get him in a hold, but would he dodge away? Could Sam be aggressive and get Purple to run? He'd expected it to go the other way. What would the partner do under any scenario? Sam nodded to the negotiator. "Thanks. Watch for a sign then get paramedics and Swat in there for the hostage." What would Partner do?

The negotiator nodded. "We call them the Incidental Rescue Squad, but I'll talk to the captain. We'll get it done."

They called Swat the IRS? Blinking, Sam walked out. At the bottom of the metal stairs, he stopped and bounced, trying to get his muscles loose and burn off the dread in his belly. As he headed for the door again, the crowd cheered. Sam put a finger to his mouth. "Ssh."

A boy, maybe eight years old, gaped and pointed. His eyes got wide, and he put hand over his mouth.

Winking at the kid, Sam made some Krav Maga moves into a playful dance. He struck a pose, but before he could elaborate on his performance, a new helicopter swooped down. It's red-white-and-blue paint job sparkled in the sun. The image of a man standing arms akimbo adorned the side, below which bright letters emblazoned the occupants as The Adventures. Who thought of that name? It was grammatically incorrect.

The chopper did not land, but hovered low enough to knock a few people down and make everyone else duck or lean into the wind. Three people jumped from five feet up, one in a business suit, the other two looking like soldiers in combat armor, complete with helmets and faceplates. The entire getup came in shades of blue, from electric to sky to cobalt. An odd metal collar on both suits created a nice contrast, right down to the yellow glowing light or gemstone right below the chin. The feds had arrived and made sure everyone knew it, especially Purple and Partner.

Folding his arms, Sam waited, tapping his foot. What could these guys do? Neither one appeared to have a weapon. Agent Jones's Favored Persons had arrived, but just for a test run? Or were they tested, vetted, and proven? Sam had never heard of the Adventures. Perhaps the silly name made people think the whole team above board.

Sam folded his arms and cocked his head as they approached. "What powers do you two have?"

Neither said a word, but the shorter one faded away, becoming invisible. The tall one pulled off a glove. His hand turned metallic and lengthened, the five fingers, held together, forming a blade. It might not cut well, but it would skewer. Then again, bullets didn't bother Purple much. Would slashing or skewering work better?

This even newer Agent Jones sauntered up behind. She had her hair dyed red, white, and blue, but tied so tight it looked brown. She wore a man's suit and had an earpiece and glasses almost as dark as her skin. She needed to join the Men in Black—or maybe they ought to join her.

She held out a hand. "Hi, I'm Agent Jones. You must be Narcolepsy. We're very interested in capturing Purple. You're sure there's a partner?"

"Positive. Purple didn't shoot me or escape on his own, since I had him in my dream." Now, Purple wanted Sam, so sending these guys in alone would get Donelle killed. "They have a woman held hostage in there. They chose her to get to me. Here's how we're going to do it. I'll knock on the door and try to get Purple to chase me. You two stay in the hallway and attack Purple from behind." The invisible man hadn't reappeared, but Sam's weird dreams came back to him. Robin Hood? "You wouldn't have a bow and arrows in that chopper, would you?"

"Hold on." Agent Jones talked into her cheek-mic. A moment later, someone tossed a five-foot long case down from the helicopter.

The Invisible Kid caught it. Either that, or it just stopped four feet off the ground. Then it vanished, showing the kid's specific control.

Sam shook his head. At least these feds came with good toys. "That will help. When Purple takes on you two, I'll go let the firemen in to get the hostage out through the window. Remember; Purple has a partner." He almost said an invisible partner, but it didn't fit. Invisible wouldn't make the officer in the van miscount. "This partner has a weird power, he makes you not notice him. This guy can sneak up on us, so watch out."

"Sounds good," Agent Jones said, though neither of the others replied.

With a sigh, Sam strode into the building and up the stairs. He hoped the invisible guy came along. Agent Jones did not. On the second floor, Sam walked into a hallway from a bombed-out building in Syria—shattered ceiling, dented and cracked concrete, torn carpet, and one dark stain. Donelle had put up a fight. Good for her, or maybe not, since she'd gotten hurt.

He walked to Donelle's door, motioned the Favored Persons a little farther down the way, and rubbed his sweaty palms on his spandex pants. What lay beyond would hurt, but he couldn't abandon her on their first monthly kidnapping. He had to rescue her so they could have a second. Sam reached up and knocked.

14
Round Two

A big bouncing rubber ball approached Donelle's closed apartment door. Sam took a deep breath, stepped to one side, closer to the favored persons. He bent his knees, and got up on his toes, ready.

A voice came from the other side. "Who's there?" The bouncing did not stop. It sounded like a kid's playground, echoing through the building.

"Narcolepsy. I heard you wanted to see me."

Purple smashed through the door, bounced off the far wall and adjusted his flight toward Sam. Dodgeball. The fight had become dodgeball in the hall near the wall. Sam had always hated that game. The Krav Maga swipe, as if hitting a thrown object, knocked Sam aside rather than Purple. Purple hit the wall, smashing sheetrock and breaking studs.

The second bounce moved Sam farther away from Donelle's door and toward the favored persons. His arm stung, like on the playground in grade school.

Right on cue, Steel Hand stepped out of a doorway and stabbed Purple as he rebounded.

Screaming, Purple bounced up, trying to land on Steel Hand. The hole in his side stopped bleeding, like a self-sealing ball. It would take a lot of wounds for Purple to bleed out. Sam slipped back toward the door and put his back against the wall. Closing his eyes, he tried to calm his breathing and listen.

Every fiber of his body wanted to dash into the apartment and rescue Donelle. He needed the partner to make a move first. Someone drew the slide on a handgun. He'd heard that sound, hanging around with Office Johns. Could the police be inside? He doubted it. No one with a handgun would do much to Purple.

A shot rang out. The bullet ricocheted on metal. The only metal would be the door frames and Steel Hand's collar. Sam opened his eyes and slipped into Donelle's apartment.

Back in the corridor, a huge crash with cracking timber and shattering concrete sounded like Purple and gone right through the damaged floor. Steel Hand cried out. A *boing* sounded from below, and Purple came back up, crashing through the floor again. Debris flew past the door.

Letting the favored persons deal with the bad guys, Sam tiptoed farther in. Purple and Jenna had trashed the apartment. Huge dents, floor and ceiling, marred the short corridor leading to the living room and kitchen. Her recliner lay in pieces, strewn across the carpet, all covered in sheetrock dust like the entire room. Someone had left the stove on, based on the burnt-potato stench.

A gunshot echoed in from the corridor. That had to be Partner, so Sam dashed for the bedroom. Donelle lay on the bed, lower leg twisted in a way a leg couldn't bend. Blood leaked onto the sheets. Before even checking on her, Sam went over and opened the window. He waved at the fireman, who stood close, waiting.

As their ladder clicked up against the sill, Sam went back to check Donelle. He touched her shoulder and kissed her forehead. "I'm here."

Donelle stirred and her eyes opened. "Oh, good. I was ahead two to one, but I had to take an injury timeout. Do you suppose I can get a rematch?"

Before Sam could reply or even make any sense of it, an EMT clambered up the ladder, followed by two firemen with a stretcher. They shoved it in and started breaking out the window.

"Where are you?" Purple shouted as he stepped in through Donelle's door.

Sam looked at the firemen. "Get her out fast." To Donelle, he said, "I'll do the rematch for you."

"Good. Sloppy leg hurts." She waved at her damaged calf even as the EMT gave her a shot and the other firemen set the stretcher on the bed

Stepping out into the living room, Sam prepared his mind for more dodgeball. Purple and Partner seemed to have dealt with Steel Hand. What had happened to the Invisible Kid, though? Now Sam had to deal with them alone. Although, Purple walked in, with blood on his costume, if it was a costume. He had a couple puncture wounds and four arrows sticking out of him. Maybe Purple needed a bicycle pump to get his mojo back.

"Here I am," Sam said. "You know this whole episode is ruining your whole Robin Hood façade, right? You hurt an innocent bystander."

"What?" Purple asked.

Sam shook his head. "This one isn't about being a pain in the ass to the rich. Robin Hood doesn't do vengeance."

"I don't care. You put me in the haunted castle." Purple breathed in, getting spherical and purple again. The arrows fell out, although from the smell, some gas still bubbled from the leaks.

Had Sam scared him? If Sam got close, would Partner risk shooting Purple? Either way. Sam charged. He ducked the first bounce, blocking with forearm. The move pushed Sam sideways again. Jumping over recliner parts, he tried to grab Purple. Sweat ran down his chest, and his wounded side ached.

Purple changed his trajectory, going up and over. Sam ducked and deflected again. He fell on his ass. With a three-corner bank shot, Purple shattered a wall, then the ceiling, and came down again. Sam rolled, and Purple went right through the floor. As the joists cracked and splintered, the remaining floor tilted until Sam fell off the edge. He caught Purple just as he started back up, doing a belly-flop onto the big ball. With a twist, Sam slipped off the side, trying to land on something soft.

He hit a sofa, and a TV remote bounced up. Sam grabbed it from the air and turned on the eighty-seven inch, high-definition screen.

More debris rained down as Purple hit Donelle's roof and came back through a different part of the floor. Sam shouted to be heard over the crashing apartment building. "Want to watch some hoops?"

Purple unfolded his legs and stopped. "What?"

Sam pointed at the screen. "We've got basketball on. Take a load off and relax."

"We're having a fight here! I'm going to squash you."

"You're no fun, and not much of a good guy either."

Ignoring Sam, Purple jumped, folding his legs and bouncing off the ceiling. Sam leaped up and tried to grab a foot before his opponent could get much momentum. Purple still lifted Sam off his feet, but he also twisted in the air, dislodging Sam. The dreams scared Purple. He also seemed hampered in close quarters.

Trying to take advantage of that, Sam backed into the short corridor of this first-floor apartment. Purple bounced a couple times then went up through the ceiling back into Donelle's apartment. It felt like an earthquake, so Sam did an earthquake drill. He opened the apartment door and stood beneath the lintel.

Purple came down in a shower of wood, plaster, and concrete right where Sam had been. Playing Purple's fear, Sam leapt at him again, trying for a hold. If he could get him into the dream…silly. Then he'd already have won.

Lunging and missing, left Sam on the ground. When Purple bounced away again, smashing the giant TV, and back, Sam kicked to his feet and dove into the hall. Another hole in the ceiling out here showed the battle Steel Hand and the Invisible Kid. Where had the kid gotten to anyway?

The rubber-ball sound Purple made went up and over. Figuring Purple would come down through the hall hole, Sam stepped back into the door again. The whole fight began to get old. Grab, bounce, hide, grab, bounce, hide. How long could this go on?

When Purple came back down Sam dodged another hardball right through the door this time and made a half-hearted grab. If he could catch the ball and throw it back, he'd win. Or not. How did you win dodgeball, against the ball? How did the end-game end? What happened if Purple knocked him out? The police said when he'd been shot, it had been point-blank range. Would Partner sneak right up to him again?

Before considering how bad an idea it might be, Sam intentionally missed the block on Purple's next bounce and threw himself backward out into the hall again. The blow sent him flying anyway and cracked a rib. He hit the carpeted floor with his own bounce and landed on some debris. He'd lost at dodgeball. Again.

When he stopped, Sam closed his eyes and lay still. He wanted to writhe in pain. He wanted to leap down the ladder to be with Donelle. He stayed quiet.

No one spoke or moved for what seemed an eternity. "You want to kill him?" Purple said.

"I do," a woman said. She walked closer, falling into Sam's trap. He hoped she chose to savor the experience. "No one messes with us and lives. If we didn't have a thousand cops outside, I'd make him hurt." Her soft, unimportant footsteps came closer.

Sam calmed his breathing, listening, trying to detect a temperature change, a wisp of air. For a moment, nothing. This woman did not matter. He smelled gun oil. Sam lashed out, striking a hand as the gun fired. The automatic clattered against the wall. Pain erupted in his ear. He grabbed her arm and pulled her onto him.

Not bothering to open his eyes, Sam relaxed and held on as the woman struggled.

"Let go!" She screamed.

Who did he have? Someone who didn't matter, maybe a bystander.

He had to protect her, though. He had to fall asleep. Sam thought back to his boss's speech at the last staff meeting. The team had to reduce costs and improve efficiency to help hold down healthcare costs. As if IT had anything to do with it.

Purple tried to pull Sam's arms free, but a rubber ball couldn't create much leverage.

Donelle's apartment faded to a dank room in an old castle decked out as a laboratory from a 1920's mad scientist movie.

The place stank like rotten eggs. No-longer-Purple lay strapped to a table. Off to one side sat a Jacob's Ladder, its bright white electrical arc climbing up over and over. On the other side, a Tesla Coil ionized the air, causing sparks and tiny lightning bolts. Another table, next to Purple's, had someone else strapped to it, but Sam paid it no mind.

Cackling, Sam rubbed his hands together in evil glee. He reached for the giant lever on the wall. His mom's voice rang through the dungeon. "There is no excuse for hurting another human being. Even the vilest sinner is made in God's image. Do you want to hurt God's image?" She never said anything of the sort in real life, preferring condemnation.

Not-Purple laughed, and Sam ground his teeth. "Yes. Yes, I do."

Rather than go for the lever, Sam pushed the button next to it. Pop! Pop! Balloons exploded. Purple and Partner tried to jump out of their bonds.

"Surprise!" Sam walked over to Not-Purple. "Tell your partner to show herself, or things will get entertaining."

Another guy appeared down by Not-Purple's feet. Expecting Sergeant Willis, Sam didn't recognize this pale, thin blond guy. "Invisible?"

"Um, you can see me? Where am I?" He'd confirmed his identity, at least. Invisible Kid wrinkled his nose. "This place smells as bad as that hallway."

Sam wanted to laugh. Instead he waved at the surroundings. "Welcome to the fun! Did they get Donelle out?"

"Yes. The paramedics are working on her."

Relieved, Sam looked around. "I think it's time to let nature take its course." Sam walked over and hit a button on the generator. A bright arc leapt up to the wooden ceiling. Beams cracked and splintered, then blew away in the wind. Rain pelted down, but only over the two beds.

"Hey!" Invisible cried out. "What are you doing?"

"Getting everyone wet." Sam turned around and walked out into the meadow where the rain stopped, leaving sparkling grass. He strode away and jumped back to face Not-Purple as a giant robot. The man needed a lesson, maybe several. "Hey, Invis, want to play catch?"

Sam tossed Not-Purple to Invisible Guy, who had also grown fifty feet or so. Invisible Guy missed, but Not-Purple didn't bounce. "We need a better bouncy ball," Invisible Guy said, tossing Not-Purple back.

Sam tossed Not-Purple between his hands. "You do like being a ball, right?"

"Wait! What?" Purple stammered.

While Sam had never messed with a person's shape, he owned this dream. He squished Not-Purple into a ball.

"Hey, stop! Wait!"

Stepping back, Sam tossed the purple ball into the air. With an overhand serve, he swatted Not-Purple over the net. Invisible Guy, with excellent form, bumped Purple back.

"Ow! Stop!"

Sam set the ball straight up, to himself, and spiked it. Invisible missed the block. Purple bounced on the grass, wailing all the way. "Time out! Time out!"

Invisible trotted over, shaking the ground with each step. "Are there timeouts in volleyball? I say we give it to him."

"You're only saying that because I'm up one-zip."

Invisible snorted as he tossed Purple back. "I want to stay here and not go back to the Adventures."

Sam dribbled Purple as they spoke. "I wondered about those metal collars. Still, how do we teach Purple here not to be a bad guy."

"Don't know. When they shot his collar, Steel Hand got away. Lucky bastard. They'll catch him again, though."

Sam pursed his lips. "Do you suppose anyone has restrained Purple and Partner yet?"

One Lego flying monkey flapped down from the sky and landed on the ball. It had Sergeant Willis's head, again. "Hi, kid. The feds are saying it's time to wake up. Think you can make this dream last a while longer, just to annoy them?"

Invisible pointed with his thumb. "I'm with him."

Sam bounced Purple a couple more times. "Why not? Sergeant, you're with the Invisible Kid there. Purple's Partner, you're on my team. The score is one-nothing." Tossing the ball, Sam hit it on the way down and lofted it over the net, wondering if Partner would participate. Purple complained again.

Sergeant Willis flew up to bump the ball to Invisible Kid, who set it high, the ball squealing with each hit, though Sam doubted it hurt. Willis spiked it from ten feet above the net. Diving, Sam got one arm beneath the ball and sent it back over the net toward the Invisible Kid. He set it too close to the net, though. The Kid spiked it. Sam couldn't get there.

The ball sailed back over the net, surprising Willis. He still managed to lob it back.

The ball yelled, "Jenna! Don't help them!"

Now, Partner had a name, Jenna, not to mention a confirmed gender. This time, Sam didn't even try for it. He waited for the ball to go back over the net, but it didn't. Everyone stood around for a bit, expecting something to happen.

"Are you going to serve?" Willis asked.

"Um,' Sam muttered. "I don't have the ball. Shit, Jenna took it."

"Who's Jenna?" Invisible Guy asked.

Shrinking down to his regular self, Sam sat on the grass and laughed. The other two looked confused until Sam recovered. "You know the idea about staying here a while? I think Jenna just arranged it." He looked around. Where would Jenna take her partner? Where *could* she take him?

Sam stood and brushed off his pants, even though no dream grass had stuck to them. "We're going back to the lab."

The Invisible Guy looked around. "Where is it?"

"This way." Sam walked off the volleyball court, through the damp meadow and into the lab, empty besides the Jacob's Ladder and Tesla Coil. The air still smelled bad.

"Cool, if stinky," Willis said, looking around. "Where's our ball?"

"Good question. The only other place is the haunted castle." Sam walked through the iron-bound door and climbed the stairs.

The higher they went, the less it stank and the brighter the colors of the walls.

"What are these walls made of?" Invisible Guy asked.

Someone high above cackled. "Fly, my pretties! Fly!" Sam wondered if they'd heard Jenna, or if the Lego Witch had spotted Purple.

On command, Sergeant Willis took wing, rising up the spiral stairwell. He yelled back down. "Legos." Willis crashed through the tower ceiling. Brown plastic bricks rained down on Sam and Invisible. A little Krav Maga knocked them aside.

"Ow!" Invisible Kid shouted. "Stop that! Ouch!"

Sam rolled his eyes and continued on up. "What do they do with you in the Adventures?"

"Man, I hate that name. It's stupid. We train, sometimes together. They don't tell us jack shit. Those collars make us obey orders. No idea how it works."

They emerged on a dark balcony, looking out over the Lego haunted forest of sharp, black, plastic branches. Willis flapped his plastic wings and landed on the parapet. "I don't see them out there, Kid."

The witch cackled again, but Sam didn't see anyone. What would happen if someone stayed in the dream when he woke up? Nothing good. "Hey, you two! The three of us are waking up. Come along, or I'm not responsible for what happens to you in here."

From down in the trees, some indistinct voices drifted up. Much louder, Purple said, "I'm not staying here! You have no idea what that haunted castle is like. I don't care if the feds have caught us."

"Sounds like he's ready," Willis said.

The sound of a kicked ball reached them, and Purple sailed up toward the tower. He flew too high, bouncing off the Lego-slate roof. Willis flapped up after the ball, catching it on the way back down.

"Hey! Let go," Purple screamed.

"Relax, I'm a good flying monkey."

Willis brought the purple ball over to Sam, who bounced it a couple times before grabbing it and stretching.

"Ow! Stop that. That hurts."

Invisible Guy rolled his eyes. "He complains when you make him into a ball and complains when you stretch him out again. Give it a rest."

"He can't help but rest," Sam said. "We're asleep."

Not-Purple popped back to his normal size and shook the kinks out. "Can we get out of here? And I'm still a good guy."

"Sure, although a good guy would give all the money away." Sam turned to the forest again. "Jenna, please come. You might die if you stay here when I wake up."

Not-Purple shook his head. "She refuses to live in a cage. She'd rather die."

The sunrise out beyond the trees caught his attention and another old church song about kneeling at dawn came to mind. "Everyone, kneel and hold hands."

"What?" the Invisible Kid said. "That makes no sense."

"I'm with him" Purple said.

On his knees, Sam held out his hands. "It's my dream, guys. Does any of this make sense? Do you want to wake up or not?"

That got them moving. Soon he had a circle with hands clasped. "Let's go for a ride." The tower's floor collapsed and the four of them slid down a Lego chute. They landed hard, waking. He needed to get over this falling thing.

Sam opened his eyes on the ruined apartment. He had to get to Donelle.

15
Play it Again, Sam

Sam couldn't breathe. He had three people lying on him. "Off!" he croaked. He couldn't hear in one ear.

The Invisible Guy faded as he rose. Purple, with handcuffs and a metal collar on his neck, rolled over and pressed something into Sam's hand. Then he climbed to his feet looking relieved and annoyed at the same time. Jenna didn't move. Sam could see her now. He blinked, a chill running through him. Her power worked inside his dream. Why? No one else's did.

Some police officers pulled Jenna free and Sam jumped up. His ribs and side objected, not to mention a few dozen other bruises, but he had to find Donelle. He ran and limped toward the stairwell and out, hurdling chunks of concrete and wood. Emerging from the door, which now hung on one hinge due to a snapped frame, he ignored the cops and the crowd who cheered him on. He had to dash across the parking lot. The ambulance started to pull out as he banged on the back. An EMT opened the door, and Sam jumped in without asking permission. "Will she be okay?"

"You came for me?" Donelle asked, her voice slurred from pain meds.

Sam crawled over opposite the EMT and took Donelle's hand. "I did. I let the firemen in and caught Purple and his partner too."

"Oh. Okay. I beat him at volleyball."

"Um…" Sam had no idea how to reply. If he didn't know better, he'd have thought she joined them in his dream. Glancing out the ambulance's back window, he saw the feds loading Jenna's stretcher into their helicopter. Purple climbed in after, deflated and tame in his Federal slave collar.

Sam glanced at what Purple had given him—a USB stick. After thinking about what it might contain, he looked across at the EMT. "Will she be okay?"

The guy shrugged. "Her shin is crushed, I suspect some ligament damage in her knee too. She'll have a long road back, lots of therapy."

"Sloppy!" Donelle slurred. "Ray said sloppy." She gestured at her bandaged and splinted shin. "Bad, sloppy leg!"

Chuckling, Sam leaned over and kissed her luscious lips through his spandex mask. "I like your legs."

She grabbed his costume and pulled him close. "Ssh. It's a secret. I like them too, but the first monthly kidnapping, no fun."

Kissing her forehead, Sam leaned back, groaning a little when his cracked rib caught, and held her hand as the ambulance, sirens blaring, passed stopped cars and screamed around corners. Last time, it had been him on the gurney. Donelle had said first. That meant, even hopped up on pain meds, she anticipated a second.

~~~~

Two weeks and three surgeries later, Donelle hobbled into Sam's apartment on crutches while he held the door. She took one look at the little place, gasped, and fell against him while trying to turn around. She twisted and kissed him.

When they came up for air, Donelle laid a hand on his cheek. "You brought my stuff!"

He'd brought over so much! Five plants, her bedspread, pillows, pans, plates, and clothes displacing some of his in the closet. The police said her building had been condemned. How had Sam gotten in?

Setting her back on her feet, well crutches, Sam helped her move into the room. "Officer Johns and Sergeant Willis helped me box and move it all. I got a storage unit too, for some of my stuff and whatever wouldn't fit."

"You..." Donelle kissed him again. What a thoughtful and earnest man, so unlike her ex-husband. "If I could move my leg, I'd jump your bones right now."

Sam laughed. "You forget who your lover is. Come, let's cuddle." He helped her to the bed and laid her on her back. He set her crutches against the wall where she could get to them before scooting in beside her, putting his leg across her good one and his arm across her chest.

He couldn't sleep when he tried, and today she wanted him asleep. So rather than flirt, Donelle vented about work. "I talked to the partners. I hate letting them down, but they put me on short-term disability. I'll have a job when I get back, but I'd rather be working."

"Right now, getting well is most important. I went through your office, too. Nell helped me. Now, if I can just stay awake long enough. The stuff in your fridge and cupboards didn't fare well. With all the things I brought over, we can sort what goes where later." Then he stammered a bit. "There is one other thing. Purple gave me the access codes to his Panama bank accounts. I donated half and created an anonymous non-profit to fight the Favored Persons Act. Does that make me a bad guy?"

He hadn't given the money back to the banks, and worried it made him a bad guy, but he hadn't kept it either. Sam's eyes drooped. Donelle grinned and relaxed. She'd grown to love his droopy eyes.

~~~~

They walked along the beach together. Donelle leaned against Sam's arm. Again, it didn't smell at all, no odor, since he'd still never been to a beach. Missing the rotting-seaweed stench, Donelle also found herself glad not to smell it.

"I have a better idea." Sam turned left, walking up a path inlaid with paving stones between two dunes. Ahead, a circle of blooming apricot trees covered the grassy dell with white petals and the air with a sweet aroma. He had some style and some romance in his blood.

Donelle smiled and kissed him. He laid her on the soft, fragrant ground and their clothes vanished. She wiggled beneath him. "Mmm. This is…ow!" The petals turned to dry leaves and sticks. From nearby, but outside the trees, laughter peeled. "What the hell, Sam?"

"It wasn't me." He sat up and looked around. "Jenna! Stop it!"

Sam had told her Jenna had stayed behind and that her power worked in the dreams. Donelle got a wicked idea, since Sam required touch. She raised an eyebrow at Sam and winked. "Hey, Jenna? How about a threesome?"

The End

Acknowledgements and Dedication

Please remember to leave a review for this book at your favorite retailer.

~~~~

This book is dedicated to my friends at 3t Systems who first suggested that falling asleep could be a super power. Plus, my wife, who is always supporting and encouraging, deserves a shout out in every book. Thank you one and all.

~~~~

Visit my web site at:
http://www.richardfriesen.net

If you like my stories, consider becoming a patron to help me with the costs of editing and cover art. You also get early access to stories and inside information on what I'm doing:
https://www.patreon.com/richardfriesen

~~~~

Look for **The Dreaming King Saga** in your favorite online bookstore now:
The Tower of Dreams
Oathbound Sisters
An Uncivil War
On Black Mesa
The Gates of Heaven

~~~~

Coming Soon:

Narcolepsy Falls Asleep – 108

Narcolepsy is Shocked
Prodigy (Part one of the Clark Family Legend)

~~~~

These professionals all did wonderful work on this book:
Editing: Courtney Farrell

~~~~

Cover Art: Abel Daniel-Florin
https://99designs.com/profiles/1438467

~~~~

Made in the USA
Columbia, SC
29 May 2020